All's Faire
in Middle School

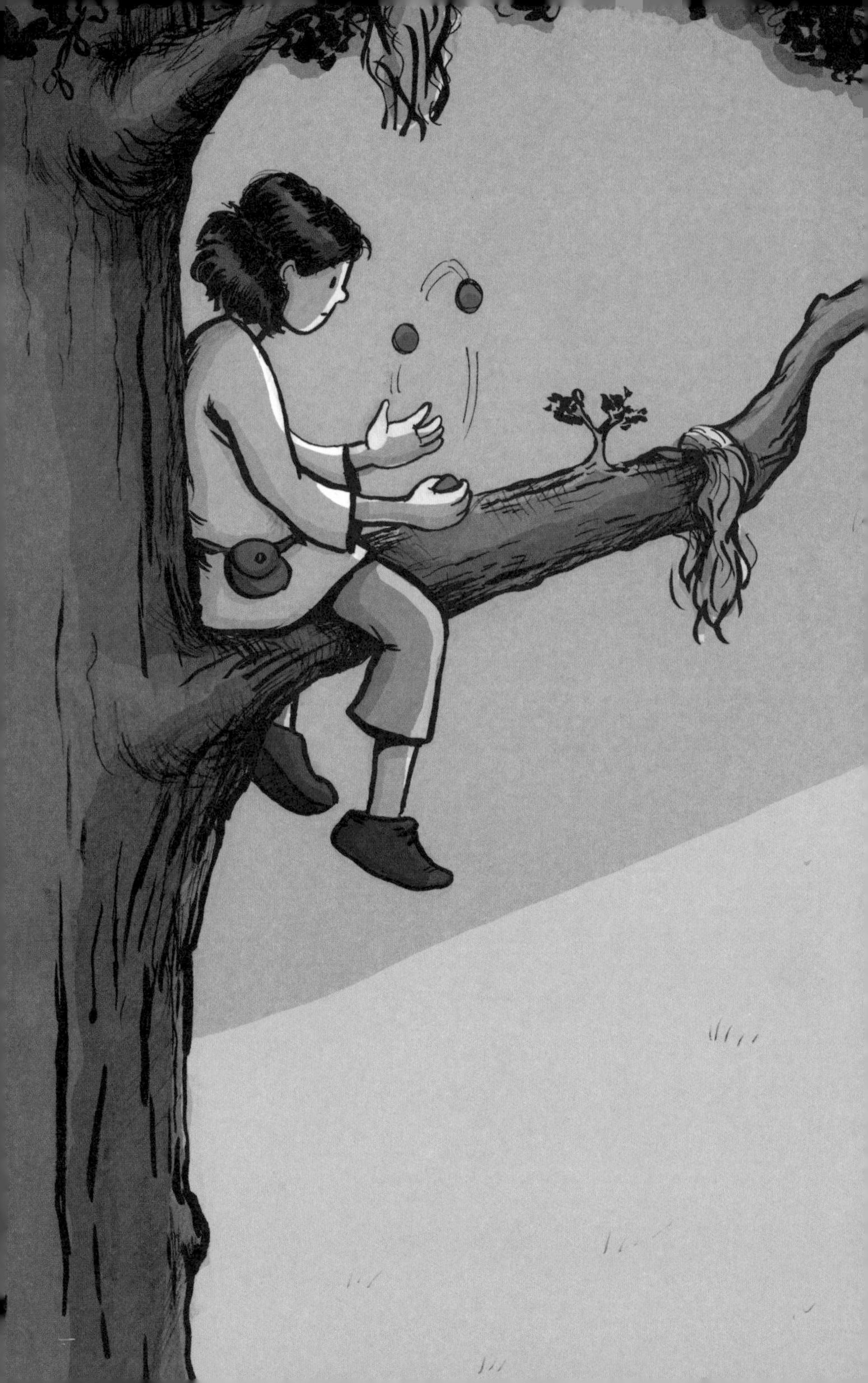

IMOGENE! HASTEN DOWN FROM THAT TREE! HER MAJESTY THE QUEEN REQUESTS YOUR PRESENCE!

THE QUEEN? ME?

THY NAME IS IMOGENE, IS IT NOT? MAKE HASTE, YOU MUSTN'T KEEP HER MAJESTY WAITING!

MOTHER! MOTHER! THE QUEEN WISHES TO SEE ME!

...WHAT HAPPENED TO YOU?

I FELL IN THE MUD PIT!

WELL, YOU'D BEST HURRY ALONG. WE'LL FOLLOW BEHIND.

MUSTN'T KEEP HER MAJESTY WAITING!

RUN, LASS!

METHINKS SHE PLANS ON THROWING YOU IN THE STOCKS!

AH! THERE'S THE QUEEN.

CLANG!

CLANG!

WHACK!

FATHER! ARE YOU ALL RIGHT?

BIT OF A WHACK ON THE SKULL, BUT 'TIS ONLY MY BRAINS AFTER ALL, AND WE KNOW I HAVEN'T MUCH OF **THOSE**.

WELL FOUGHT, BRAVE KNIGHTS. I SHALL NOW RETIRE TO MY CHAMBERS; THE HEAT DOTH OVERTAKE ME AT THE MOMENT.

BEGGING YOUR PARDON, YOUR MAJESTY. YOU WISHED TO SEE ME?

AH YES. YOUNG LADY IMOGENE. I HAVE HEARD TOLD YOU HAVE RECENTLY TURNED ELEVEN YEARS OF AGE AND WISH TO START TRAINING AS A SQUIRE.

INDEED, YOUR MAJESTY!

ARE YOU SURE THOU ART OLD ENOUGH TO SERVE MY KINGDOM? MY SQUIRES MUST BE VERY BRAVE INDEED. TELL ME, YOUNG LADY...HOW WILST THOU PROVE THY COURAGE?

WITH YOUR MAJESTY'S LEAVE, I HAVE PREPARED AN EXTREMELY TREACHEROUS QUEST TO PROVE MY STRENGTH AND COURAGE!

INDEED? AND WHERE SHALL THIS EXTREMELY TREACHEROUS QUEST TAKE YOU?

I SHALL GO...

DIAL BOOKS FOR YOUNG READERS
PENGUIN YOUNG READERS GROUP · AN IMPRINT OF PENGUIN RANDOM HOUSE LLC
375 HUDSON STREET, NEW YORK, NY 10014

COPYRIGHT © 2017 BY VICTORIA JAMIESON

PRINTED IN CHINA
HC ISBN 9780525429982 / 10 9 8 7 6 5 4 3 2 1
PB ISBN 9780525429999 / 10 9 8 7 6 5 4 3 2 1

COLOR BY DAVID LASKY · DESIGN BY VICTORIA JAMIESON AND JASON HENRY

All's Faire in Middle School

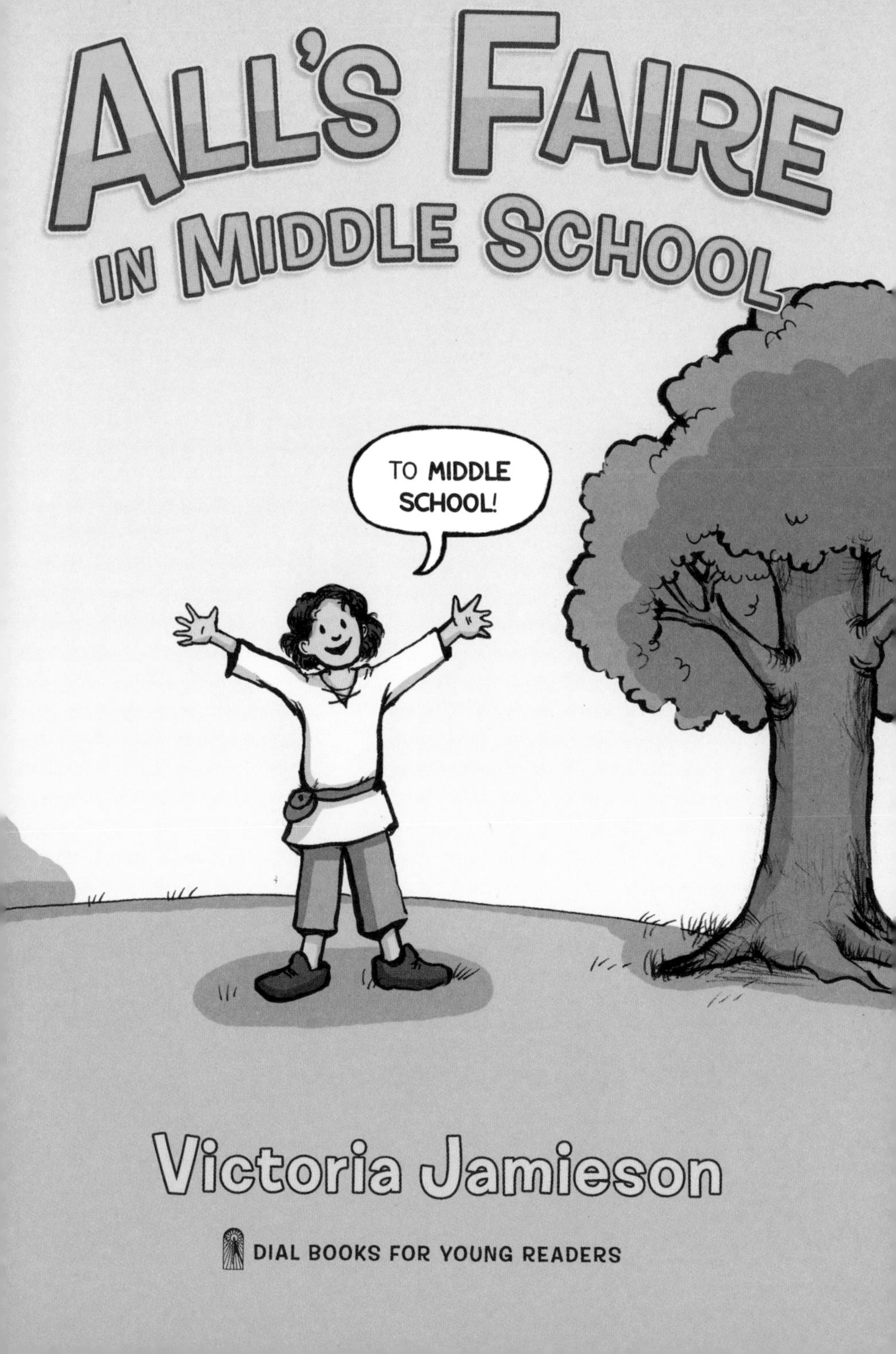
TO MIDDLE SCHOOL!

Victoria Jamieson

DIAL BOOKS FOR YOUNG READERS

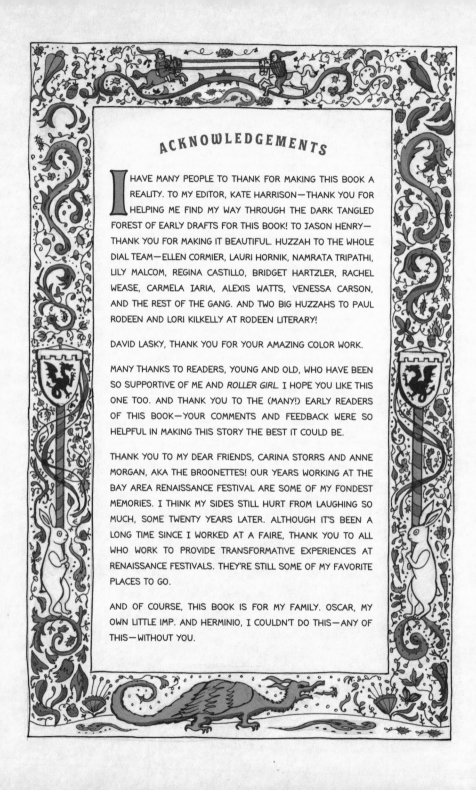

ACKNOWLEDGEMENTS

I HAVE MANY PEOPLE TO THANK FOR MAKING THIS BOOK A REALITY. TO MY EDITOR, KATE HARRISON—THANK YOU FOR HELPING ME FIND MY WAY THROUGH THE DARK TANGLED FOREST OF EARLY DRAFTS FOR THIS BOOK! TO JASON HENRY— THANK YOU FOR MAKING IT BEAUTIFUL. HUZZAH TO THE WHOLE DIAL TEAM—ELLEN CORMIER, LAURI HORNIK, NAMRATA TRIPATHI, LILY MALCOM, REGINA CASTILLO, BRIDGET HARTZLER, RACHEL WEASE, CARMELA IARIA, ALEXIS WATTS, VENESSA CARSON, AND THE REST OF THE GANG. AND TWO BIG HUZZAHS TO PAUL RODEEN AND LORI KILKELLY AT RODEEN LITERARY!

DAVID LASKY, THANK YOU FOR YOUR AMAZING COLOR WORK.

MANY THANKS TO READERS, YOUNG AND OLD, WHO HAVE BEEN SO SUPPORTIVE OF ME AND *ROLLER GIRL*. I HOPE YOU LIKE THIS ONE TOO. AND THANK YOU TO THE (MANY!) EARLY READERS OF THIS BOOK—YOUR COMMENTS AND FEEDBACK WERE SO HELPFUL IN MAKING THIS STORY THE BEST IT COULD BE.

THANK YOU TO MY DEAR FRIENDS, CARINA STORRS AND ANNE MORGAN, AKA THE BROONETTES! OUR YEARS WORKING AT THE BAY AREA RENAISSANCE FESTIVAL ARE SOME OF MY FONDEST MEMORIES. I THINK MY SIDES STILL HURT FROM LAUGHING SO MUCH, SOME TWENTY YEARS LATER. ALTHOUGH IT'S BEEN A LONG TIME SINCE I WORKED AT A FAIRE, THANK YOU TO ALL WHO WORK TO PROVIDE TRANSFORMATIVE EXPERIENCES AT RENAISSANCE FESTIVALS. THEY'RE STILL SOME OF MY FAVORITE PLACES TO GO.

AND OF COURSE, THIS BOOK IS FOR MY FAMILY. OSCAR, MY OWN LITTLE IMP. AND HERMINIO, I COULDN'T DO THIS—ANY OF THIS—WITHOUT YOU.

CHAPTER ONE

HI.

ur story begins here... at the beginning. Our heroine Imogene does not know it yet, but her journey through the dark and treacherous woods of Middle School shall be a twisty path indeed...

DAD

MOM

TIFFANY

FELIX

UGGH, YOU ARE BRAVE. MIDDLE SCHOOL IS THE **WORST**.

TERRIBLE PLACE, MIDDLE SCHOOL!

WORST YEARS OF MY LIFE.

THANKS FOR THE VOTE OF CONFIDENCE, EVERYBODY! AREN'T ADULTS SUPPOSED TO, YOU KNOW, **ENCOURAGE** KIDS TO GO TO SCHOOL?

YOU GOT THE WRONG KIND OF GROWN-UPS, KID. WHAT HAPPENED TO **YOU**?

I FELL IN THE MUD PIT AGAIN ON OUR WAY OVER HERE!

MOM! DID YOU HEAR? I GET TO START TRAINING TO BE A **SQUIRE**!

I HEARD, IMPY. MY LITTLE GIRL IS GROWING UP!

SIGH

MOM, **STOP**!

MY FAMILY HAS WORKED AT THE FLORIDA RENAISSANCE FAIRE EVER SINCE I WAS A BABY. UP UNTIL NOW, ALL I **REALLY** GOT TO DO WAS HANG AROUND THE SHOPPE AND HELP MY MOM. AND BABYSIT FELIX. BUT NOW, AS A **SQUIRE**, I'D BE AN ACTUAL CAST MEMBER!

DO I GET TO BE IN THE JOUST? HOW ABOUT THE HUMAN CHESS MATCH? HEY, AND WHEN DO I GET **PAID**?

YOUNG LADY, DO NOT FORGET THAT YOU ARE STILL IN TRAINING. YOU MUST PROVE YOUR WORTH BEFORE PERFORMING FOR THE PUBLIC.

AS FOR YOUR PAY... TWENTY DOLLARS A WEEK IS THE APPRENTICE RATE.

TWENTY BUCKS A WEEK? I'M GONNA BE **RICH**!

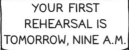

YOUR FIRST REHEARSAL IS TOMORROW, NINE A.M.

YES, YOUR MAJESTY. THANK YOU, YOUR MAJESTY!

LOOK WHAT IIIIIII HAVE!

AWWWWWW!

IMOGENE, PUT THAT AWAY OR I WILL TAKE IT FROM YOU. COME ON, LET'S LEAVE YOUR DAD TO FINISH REHEARSALS.

M'LADY.

KISS

BAAAARF!

GROW UP, YOU TWO. IMPY, LET'S GET THE REST OF YOUR BACK-TO-SCHOOL SHOPPING OVER WITH.

YIPPPPEEEEEEE!

MOM AND I ALREADY GOT NOTEBOOKS AND PENCILS AND STUFF AT VALU-MART, BUT SHE ALSO PROMISED ME TWO VERY IMPORTANT BACK-TO-SCHOOL NECESSITIES FROM THE FAIRE...

FIRST, I NEEDED A GOOD LUCK CHARM.

CRYSTALS ARE VERY POWERFUL STONES. THEY BRING THE ENERGY OF THE STARS TO THE SOUL.

SO, IT'LL BRING ME LUCK, RIGHT?

AND LAST BUT NOT LEAST, FROM THE TANNERY...

MY NEW BOOTS! SO PREEETTTY!

REMEMBER, WEAR THEM AS OFTEN AS POSSIBLE TO GET THE LEATHER SOFT AND BUTTERY. AND IF SHE STARTS TO OUTGROW 'EM, BRING 'EM BACK—I CAN STRETCH OUT THE LEATHER.

TAKE GOOD CARE OF THESE, IMPY. THEY ARE WORKS OF ART.

I KNOW, I LOVE THEM!

THESE BOOTS COST $140 AND I PAID FOR HALF OF THEM, SO YOU BET I'D TAKE GOOD CARE OF THEM.

I WANT NEW BOOOOOTS! HOW COME IMPY GETS EVERYTHING?

WE JUST GOT YOU THOSE NEW SNEAKERS, REMEMBER? BESIDES, IMPY IS GOING TO SCHOOL, SO SHE NEEDS THEM.

WHY CAN'T I GO TO SCHOOL? HUH? HUH? HUH?

I DON'T KNOW IF TEACHERS GET PAID ENOUGH FOR THAT.

WHAT DOES THAT MEAN?!

SHHH. IT JUST MEANS I GET TO KEEP YOU AROUND A FEW YEARS LONGER, OK?

OK.

I LIKE IT BETTER HERE ANYWAY.

IT **IS** NICE AROUND THE SHIRE, ESPECIALLY ON DAYS LIKE TODAY. OPENING DAY ISN'T UNTIL NEXT WEEK, SO FOR NOW IT'S JUST US RENNIES.

THESE ARE MY FAVORITE DAYS, BECAUSE YOU CAN ALMOST BELIEVE YOU'VE SLIPPED BACK IN TIME.

I'VE BEEN HOMESCHOOLED MY ENTIRE LIFE, AND IT'S PRETTY FUN GOING TO SCHOOL AT A RENAISSANCE FAIRE.

PE

BIOLOGY

SEVENTEEN PENCE IS THY CHANGE.

MATH

ENGLISH

UNO...DOS... **TRES!**

SPANISH

AND OF COURSE, HISTORY!

...AND ALL THE ARTS AND CRAFTS I CAN HANDLE AT MY MOM'S STORE.

BUT WHEN YOU'RE SURROUNDED BY DOLLS AND BEARS AND FAIRY TALES ALL DAY, IT CAN FEEL, WELL...BABYISH.

AND WHEN YOUR ONLY CLASSMATE IS A DEMENTED SIX-YEAR-OLD, YOU KNOW YOU HAVE PROBLEMS.

I MADE TIFFANY A NEW SCARF. ISN'T SHE BEEEAAUUUUTIFUL??

I THINK IT'S TIME I MET SOME KIDS WHO **DIDN'T** HAVE A STUFFED SQUIRREL FOR A BEST FRIEND.

HERE COMES YOUR FATHER. LET'S HEAD ON HOME—WE HAVE SOME MORE WREATHS TO FINISH UP TONIGHT.

OUTSIDE OF FAIRE, WE LEAD A NORMAL LIFE.

PUT THAT BACK.

IMPY, GO GET SOME TOILET PAPER, PLEASE. THE ONE ON SALE.

"NORMAL" BEING A RELATIVE TERM, OF COURSE.

I'M HAVING A BABY.

OH, HOW CUTE. IS IT A BOY OR A GIRL?

IT'S A SQUIRREL! HER NAME IS TIFFANY.

I WONDER WHAT IT WILL BE LIKE, BEING SURROUNDED BY **ACTUAL** NORMAL PEOPLE ALL DAY.

OH NO! MY WATER BROKE! THIS BABY IS COMING **NOW**!

I HOPE THAT GIRL WON'T BE IN MY CLASS AT SCHOOL...

WE LIVE IN A PRETTY NORMAL APARTMENT...

SORT OF.

MOM, I'M PUTTING MY BOOTS AWAY!

MY ROOM IS PRETTY NORMAL.
FIRST DAY OF SCHOOL OUTFIT: NORMAL.
BACKPACK: NORMAL.
EVERYTHING'S READY. I THINK. I HOPE.

ONLY A FEW DAYS TO GO UNTIL I FIND OUT.

ALLOW ME TO BUY YOU LUNCH WITH THIS CRISP $20 BILL, NEW FRIENDS!

I HEARD SHE'S A **KNIGHT**!

COOL!

WOW, NICE BOOTS!

CHAPTER TWO

Squires are not, of course, distracted by fears about popularity or other such poppycock. And so, our heroine puts these petty distractions behind her as she begins training in the Knight's Code of Honesty, Chivalry, and Bravery...and swordplay.

HIYAHH! HIYAHH!

HEE-HEE!

HI-YAHH!

WAAA-AAAA!

HEY YOU TWO! KNOCK IT OFF! IT'S EIGHT O'CLOCK IN THE MORNING—WE HAVE NEIGHBORS!

SHE DID THAT ON PURPOSE AND SHE RUINED MY SWORD!

IMPY, WHY DO YOU ALWAYS HAVE TO SET HIM OFF LIKE THAT? FELIX, PLAY YOUR VIDEO GAME. IMPY, TAKE THESE BOXES DOWN TO THE CAR, PLEASE.

HOW COME **I** HAVE TO...

YOU KNOW HOW THERE ARE SOME MYTHOLOGICAL CREATURES THAT CAN TURN THEIR VICTIMS TO STONE, JUST WITH A LOOK?

OKAY, OKAY, I'M GOING! SHEESH.

WHAT DID YOU SAY?

SHE IS GETTING SO LIPPY. I DON'T KNOW **WHAT** IS GOING ON WITH HER.

MOM GAVE **ME** A RING POP!

BIG WHOOP.

WE HELPED CARRY THE BOXES TO THE SHOPPE WHEN WE ARRIVED.

COME ON, IMPS—REHEARSALS START IN TEN MINUTES.

HAVE FUN STAYING IN THE STORE ALL DAY, LOSER!

THE SUNDAY BEFORE OPENING DAY IS ALWAYS AN ALL-CAST MEETING. BY NOW, ALL OF THE ACTORS HAD TO BE IN TOWN.

THERE ARE LOTS OF DIFFERENT RENAISSANCE FAIRES AROUND THE COUNTRY. SOME FOLKS STAY PUT AND ONLY WORK THIS ONE, LIKE MY FAMILY. SOME PEOPLE TRAVEL FROM FAIRE TO FAIRE, SO WE ONLY GET TO SEE THEM ONCE A YEAR. WHEN EVERYONE COMES BACK TO TOWN, IT'S LIKE A BIG FAMILY REUNION. A FAIRE-MILY REUNION.

WELL, WHO IS THIS GIANT BEFORE ME!

HI CUSSIE.

CUSSIE IS LIKE MY THIRD GRANDMA. EXCEPT SHE'S A LOT WEIRDER THAN MY TWO REAL GRANDMAS.

GOOD TO SEE YOU TOO, HUGO, THOU FUSTY ONION-EYED FLAP-DRAGON!

GETTING INTO TROUBLE ALREADY, CUSSIE? IT'S NIGH NINE O'CLOCK IN THE MORNING—A BIT EARLY FOR FIGHTS, EVEN FOR **YOU**!

HEY, KIT! IMPY, YOUR BETROTHED IS HERE!

DAD! **STOP**!

MAKE ONE LITTLE COMMENT WHEN YOU'RE SEVEN YEARS OLD ABOUT HOW YOU WANT TO MARRY A CERTAIN PERSON WHEN YOU GROW UP, AND NOBODY LETS YOU FORGET IT.

LADY IMOGENE! YOU GROW MORE BEAUTIFUL WITH EACH PASSING YEAR!

HOW'S MY FUTURE PERFORMANCE PARTNER? LET'S SEE HOW MUCH YOU'VE PRACTICED THIS YEAR.

OK!

KIT HAS ALWAYS SAID THAT WHEN I GET OLDER, WE'LL FORM A JUGGLING AND SWORD-FIGHTING ACT AND TOUR FAIRES AROUND THE COUNTRY. I DON'T **REALLY** THINK THAT WILL HAPPEN...STILL, IT'S NICE TO HAVE A BACKUP PLAN IF THIS MIDDLE SCHOOL THING DOESN'T PAN OUT.

WELL DONE! NEXT WE'LL WORK ON GETTING YOU UP TO **FOUR** OBJECTS.

LORDS AND LADIES, FOOLS AND JESTERS, IF YOU ARE READY, WE SHALL BEGIN!

AYE, BEGIN ALREADY, THOU QUALLING TOAD-SPOTTED CLACK-DISH!

CUSSIE GOT HER NICKNAME FOR A REASON.

WELCOME TO THE TWENTIETH ANNUAL FLORIDA RENAISSANCE FAIRE!

HUZZAH!

A FEW HOUSEKEEPING ITEMS. LIKE EVERY YEAR, THE FAIRE IS OPEN FROM TEN A.M. TO FIVE P.M., WEEKENDS ONLY, FOR EIGHT WEEKS.

THE QUEEN WENT ON WITH MORE DETAILS. I SAW LOTS OF PEOPLE I RECOGNIZED FROM OTHER YEARS. THERE'S THE MUSICIANS... THE JESTERS...THE WELL WENCHES...MUG MAN...PAULO THE CAT TRAINER...IT WAS NICE TO SEE EVERYONE AGAIN.

NOW! WHAT YOU'VE ALL BEEN WAITING FOR. AS YOU KNOW, EACH YEAR WE CHOOSE A THEME THAT RUNS THROUGH ALL OF OUR PROGRAMMING, FROM THE OPENING CEREMONIES, TO THE CHESS MATCH, TO THE JOUST.

THIS YEAR'S THEME IS—**ST. GEORGE AND THE DRAGON**!

I'D LIKE TO INTRODUCE YOU TO OUR PRINCIPAL ACTORS! PLAYING THE HERMIT, WHO EMERGES FROM HER CAVE FOR THE FIRST TIME IN FORTY-SEVEN YEARS TO WARN THE VILLAGERS...CUSSIE!

CUSSIE USUALLY GETS ONE OF THE BEST ROLES BECAUSE SHE'S SO FUNNY.

PLAYING THE EVIL LORD OF THE DRAGONS... SIR HUGO!

DAD PRETTY MUCH PLAYS THE VILLAIN EVERY YEAR. I USED TO WONDER WHY HE NEVER GETS TO PLAY THE **GOOD** KNIGHT, BUT I GUESS I'M USED TO IT BY NOW.

PLAYING OUR KIND MAIDEN PRINCESS, WHO SACRIFICES HERSELF TO THE DRAGON FOR THE GOOD OF THE KINGDOM...LADY VIOLET!

HUH, I'VE NEVER SEEN HER BEFORE— SHE MUST BE A NEW CAST MEMBER.

AND LAST BUT NOT LEAST, PLAYING SIR GEORGE IS, WHO ELSE BUT...

IT IS I, SIR GEORGE! AND **I** SHALL SLAY THIS DRAGON!

KIT PLAYS THE HERO PRETTY MUCH EVERY YEAR. HE'S CUTE AND FUNNY AND KNOWS HOW TO JUGGLE—SO YEAH, IT'S A NO-BRAINER.

IMPRESSED, PRINCESS?

IMPRESSED? IMPRESSED BY WHAT, YOU HAVEN'T DONE ANYTHING YET! I'VE SEEN MORE IMPRESSIVE STUNTS AT HER ROYAL HIGHNESS'S DOG SHOW.

AND THERE YOU HAVE IT. THAT CONCLUDES OUR MEETING. PLEASE MEET WITH YOUR GUILDS FOR MORNING REHEARSALS.

KISS

TOSS

READY TO GO, IMPS?

YEAH. WHERE DO WE GO FIRST?

I'M GOING TO SWORD-FIGHTING REHEARSALS. YOU'RE MEETING WITH CUSSIE THIS MORNING.

I AM? I THOUGHT I'D JUST HANG OUT WITH YOU ALL DAY.

YOU'RE A FULL-FLEDGED CAST MEMBER NOW. YOU HAVE YOUR OWN REHEARSALS AND DAILY SCHEDULE.

OH.

THIS WAS UNEXPECTED—BUT A LITTLE EXCITING, I GUESS, TO BE ON MY OWN!

CUSSIE WILL EXPLAIN ALL. I'LL SEE YOU THIS AFTERNOON FOR JOUST REHEARSALS.

AH! THE FIRST DAY OF REHEARSALS! A GLORIOUS DAY IN EVERY YOUNG MAIDEN'S LIFE! COME, STEP INTO MY OFFICE.

THIS WILL BE YOUR DAILY
SCHEDULE DURING THE FAIRE.
KEEP IT HANDY.

10 A.M.: GATE OPENING
CEREMONY
10:30–11:30: STREET
11:30: MIDDAY PARADE
12: HUMAN CHESS
MATCH
1–1:30 P.M.: LUNCH
1:30–4: STREET
4: JOUST
5 P.M.: GATE CLOSING
CEREMONY

WHAT DOES THIS
MEAN—"STREET"?

WE'LL GET TO THAT,
HOLD YOUR HORSES.
YOU ARE JOINING THE CAST
AS A SQUIRE, CORRECT? WHAT
WOULD YOU SAY IS YOUR MOST
IMPORTANT JOB AS A SQUIRE?

UM, WELL—HELPING
MY KNIGHT IN
COMBAT, KEEPING
THE ARMOR CLEAN...

WRONG. YOUR **MOST** IMPORTANT JOB IS TO
INTERACT WITH THE PUBLIC.

HUH?

LET ME ASK YOU
SOMETHING. WHAT
DO **YOU** LIKE BEST
ABOUT FAIRE?

WELL...IT'S **FUN.** I GET TO RUN AROUND AND
PRETEND I'M IN A DIFFERENT TIME. AND EAT
GOOD FOOD AND WATCH SHOWS AND...

YES, **PRETENDING**. THAT, MY DEAR, IS "STREET." WALKING, TALKING, AND **LIVING** AS THOUGH YOU ARE IN A RENAISSANCE VILLAGE. WE WANT GUESTS TO BE TRANSPORTED TO ANOTHER TIME SO THEY CAN FORGET ABOUT REAL LIFE FOR A LITTLE WHILE.

COME WITH ME.

GOOD MORROW, AND WELL MET, BAKER! PRITHEE, HAST THOU ANY FRESH LOAVES THIS MORNING, PERHAPS **WITHOUT** SAND OR ROCKS? I NEARLY CHIPPED A TOOTH ON THE LOAF YOU DID GIVE ME YESTERDAY!

I'M SURPRISED YE HAVE ANY TEETH LEFT, AT YOUR AGE!

HAH! YOU'RE LUCKY I HAVE THIS YOUNG LASS WITH ME, ELSE I MIGHT CALL YOU A SPLEENY BEEF-WITTED MAGGOT! FARE THEE WELL!

SEE? CONVINCE GUESTS THEY ARE IN A LIVING, BREATHING VILLAGE FILLED WITH COLORFUL CHARACTERS, AND INCLUDE THEM IN THE FUN.

MAKE THE VISITORS FEEL WELCOME, IMPY—**THAT'S** YOUR MOST IMPORTANT JOB.

WE SPENT THE REST OF THE MORNING WALKING AROUND DOING STREET. WE PRACTICED PROJECTION, WHICH IS BASICALLY SAYING THINGS **VERY LOUDLY** AND IN **A DRAMATIC FASHION**. THIS INVITES PEOPLE TO STOP AND LISTEN IF YOU'RE DOING A STREET PERFORMANCE.

WE PRACTICED THE QUEEN'S ENGLISH SOME MORE. I LEARNED SOME HELPFUL PHRASES TO SAY TO PATRONS.

28

WE ALSO PRACTICED "COLORFUL" ELIZABETHAN LANGUAGE.

THY BREATH STINKS WITH EATING TOASTED CHEESE.

THOU LUMPISH REELING-RIPE JOLT-HEAD!

THOU LOGGERHEADED RUMP-FED GIGLET!

THOU SPONGY ILL-NURTURED STRUMPET!

WELL DONE, YOU! NOW, THE HOUR STANDS 'TWIXT TWELVE AND ONE—'TIS TIME TO MEET THE OTHERS ON THE JOUSTING FIELD.

YES!!

STREET PERFORMING WAS FUN, BUT WHAT I WAS **REALLY** LOOKING FORWARD TO WAS THE JOUST. I WASN'T KIDDING MYSELF THAT THEY WOULD **ACTUALLY** LET AN ELEVEN-YEAR-OLD JOUST. BUT MAYBE I COULD BE IN THE BIG SWORD-FIGHTING SHOW AT THE END!

AH! MY SQUIRE HAST ARRIVED! HASTEN HERE, HELP ME DON MY ARMOR.

HELPING DAD FASTEN HIS ARMOR HAS ALWAYS BEEN MY SPECIAL TASK—I DO IT BETTER THAN ANYONE.

NOW, ARE YOU READY FOR YOUR TRAINING IN THE SPECIAL WEAPONS OF THE JOUST? CLOSE YOUR EYES AND STICK OUT YOUR HANDS...

SPECIAL WEAPONS?! MAYBE, JUST MAYBE...

WHAT IS **THIS** FOR?

I'LL GIVE YOU ONE GUESS.

ACTUALLY, YOU SHOULD PROBABLY GO WITH GUESS...

NUMBER TWO.

AW, MAN.

SO MY DUTIES AT THE JOUST DIDN'T END UP BEING AS GLAMOROUS AS I'D IMAGINED.

BUT I STILL HAD A **LITTLE** HOPE FOR THE BIG SWORD FIGHT AT THE END.

THE SWORD FIGHT WAS THE MOST EXCITING ONE EVER THIS YEAR. THE WOODEN DRAGON IS HOLLOW INSIDE, AND WHEN MY DAD GIVES ME THE CUE...

NOW, SQUIRE!

YANK!

...I OPEN THE HATCH, AND A BUNCH OF SOLDIERS COME POURING OUT.

AND THE FIGHT BEGINS!

OF COURSE, IN THE END, SIR GEORGE DEFEATS MY DAD, BECAUSE GOOD ALWAYS TRIUMPHS OVER EVIL.

...AND THAT CONCLUDES OUR REHEARSALS FOR THE DAY! I WILL SEE **ALL** OF YOU ON FRIDAY FOR **FULL** DRESS REHEARSAL. GOOD DAY!

WELL? HOW WAS IT?

IT WAS REALLY GOOD! THE BEST ONE EVER, I THINK!

ALTHOUGH...YOU KNOW WHAT WOULD **REALLY** MAKE THE SHOW COMPLETE, AND ADD THAT CERTAIN **JE NE SAIS QUOI**?

NICE TRY, IMPY.

I'D PRACTICE **REALLY** HARD! I **KNOW** I COULD BE GOOD ENOUGH FOR THE SHOW! BESIDES, HAVING A KID IN THE SWORD FIGHT WOULD BE EXCITING—YOU KNOW, SOMETHING NEW FOR THE FANS!

WELL, WE'LL SEE.

WHICH, AS EVERYONE KNOWS, IS PARENT FOR "NO."

AW, CHEER UP, IMP! LIKE I SAID, WE'LL SEE. TELL YOU WHAT. WE HAVE A FEW MINUTES BEFORE WE HAVE TO MEET YOUR MOM AND BROTHER. LET'S GET A PRACTICE SPAR IN.

REALLY?

NO MATTER HOW TIRED MY DAD IS, HE ALWAYS HAS TIME TO SPAR WITH ME.

WE HAVE A SPECIAL ROUTINE WE'VE WORKED OUT OVER THE YEARS. SINCE I'M SMALLER, WE USE MY SPEED AND AGILITY TO MY ADVANTAGE.

IT'S A PRETTY GOOD SHOW!

HUZZAH!

HELP YOUR OLD MAN UP, IMPY.

NOW, TAKE YOUR BOW...

AND... **SMELL MY ARMPIT**!!!

AGGH! THIS IS CHILD ABUSE! AND I HAVE ALL THESE WITNESSES!

HUH, GOOD POINT. OK, GRAB YOUR STUFF— LET'S HEAD ON HOME.

THE NEXT FEW DAYS WERE PRETTY UNEVENTFUL. I STAYED HOME AND HELPED MOM MAKE WREATHS.

AND I WORRIED.

AND CHECKED MY OUTFIT FOR SCHOOL.

AND WORRIED.

AND CHECKED MY OUTFIT.

BY TUESDAY EVENING, I WAS KIND OF A BASKET CASE.

IN EXACTLY FIFTEEN HOURS, IT WILL BE EIGHT A.M. AND I WILL BE **IN** MIDDLE SCHOOL! BY THIS TIME TOMORROW, I WILL HAVE HAD MY **FIRST DAY**! OH MAN OH MAN OH...

IMPY? UM...

I THINK YOU PUT ENOUGH RIBBONS ON THAT ONE.

WHY DON'T YOU TAKE A LITTLE BREAK? EVERYONE WILL BE HERE SOON.

OH. OK.

MIGHT AS WELL USE THIS TIME TO...

CHECK MY OUTFIT AGAIN.

34

TOMORROW MY ENTIRE LIFE WOULD CHANGE. IT WAS WEIRD THAT EVERYONE WAS GOING ABOUT THEIR BUSINESS LIKE NORMAL.

DING-DONG

AT LEAST I'LL HAVE SOME DISTRACTION TONIGHT.

DURING FAIRE SEASON, WE HAVE VISITORS OVER AT OUR HOUSE **A LOT**. I GUESS WHEN YOU'RE LIVING IN A CAMPER, EVEN SHARING A BATHROOM WITH FELIX CAN FEEL LIKE LUXURY.

HEY KIDDO, WHAT'S HAPPENING?

HAVING VISITORS ALL THE TIME IS ONE OF THE BEST PARTS OF FAIRE...

KNOCK-KNOCK!

...USUALLY.

COME IN, COME IN!

HMMMPH.

CUSSIE, HAVE YOU SEEN IMOGENE? I DON'T SEE HER ANYWHERE.

MMMFF! GEROFF ME!

SIT

KIT'S USED THIS SAME JOKE SINCE I WAS SEVEN YEARS OLD...BUT SOMEHOW IT DOESN'T BOTHER ME.

KIT! KIT! WATCH ME PLAY THIS VIDEO GAME!

WINK

I'M SORRY I DIDN'T GET TO INTRODUCE MYSELF YESTERDAY, IMOGENE. KIT'S TOLD ME ALL ABOUT YOU. I'M VIOLET.

OH. HI.

I HEAR YOU'RE STARTING MIDDLE SCHOOL TOMORROW! ARE YOU NERVOUS?

UM, A LITTLE.

WHY DID SHE HAVE TO BRING THAT UP? I WAS ENJOYING A NICE FIVE MINUTES OF NOT WORRYING ABOUT IT.

IMPY, GET OUT THE PLATES AND PAPER TOWELS—YOUR DAD WILL BE HOME SOON.

•GRUMBLE•

SO VIOLET! TELL ME HOW YOU AND KIT MET!

YOU'RE STUCK WITH ME, ALL RIGHT.

KISS

WELL...WE MET AT THE OHIO FAIRE OVER THE SUMMER, AND HE CONVINCED ME TO GO WITH HIM TO ARIZONA AND NOW, WELL...I SEEM TO BE STUCK WITH HIM!

•GAG•

I'M HOME!

PIZZA!

I DON'T KNOW WHY IT BOTHERED ME SO MUCH TO SEE KIT ALL LOVEY-DOVEY WITH HER. IT'S NOT LIKE I **REALLY** EXPECTED TO MARRY HIM SOMEDAY. BUT STILL, DO THEY HAVE TO BE **ALL OVER** EACH OTHER? IT'S GROSS.

A "WELCOME HOME, DADDY!" WOULD BE NICE.

HOT • FRESH • READY
HOT • FRESH • REA
HOT • FRESH • REA

DAD'S A LITTLE GRUMPY ON THE DAYS HE HAS TO WORK HIS OTHER JOB. WHEN HE'S NOT ON AN ACTING GIG, HE'S A SALESMAN AT PENNY PINCHER POOL SUPPLIES.

DID YOU SELL ANY JACUZZIS TO BILLIONAIRES TODAY, DADDY?

NO, BUT I SOLD SOME CHLORINE TABLETS TO SHADY OAKS RETIREMENT VILLAGE, SO THAT'S A PLUS.

CHEERS! TO HAVING THE FAIRE-MILY BACK TOGETHER!

I KNOW I'M NEW HERE, BUT I'D LIKE TO THANK YOU FOR WELCOMING ME INTO YOUR HOME. AND I'D ALSO LIKE TO PROPOSE A TOAST...TO IMOGENE! FOR STARTING A NEW AND EXCITING CHAPTER IN YOUR LIFE TOMORROW.

SHE BRINGS IT UP **AGAIN**!

AND I BROUGHT YOU A PRESENT. I KNOW THAT MIDDLE SCHOOL WAS ROUGH FOR ME, SO IT HELPED TO HAVE A PLACE TO WRITE DOWN ALL OF MY THOUGHTS.

YOU CAN WRITE ABOUT ALL OF YOUR BOYFRIENDS.

HA-HA.

THAT'S BEAUTIFUL, VIOLET! IMPY, WHAT DO YOU SAY?

THANK YOU!

I HATED TO ADMIT IT, BUT IT **WAS** BEAUTIFUL. A JOURNAL OF MY VERY OWN. IT SMELLED REALLY GOOD.

WHY DOES IMPY ALWAYS GET EVERYTHING?!

I HAVE A PRESENT FOR YOU, TOO! I BROUGHT SOME ACORNS FOR TIFFANY.

NOM NOM NOM!

WHY WAS MIDDLE SCHOOL SO BAD FOR YOU?

WELL...

THIS STARTED A BIG DISCUSSION OF...

BULLIES.

MEAN KIDS.

CLIQUES.

FIGHTS.

I GUESS KIT NOTICED THE LOOK OF ABJECT TERROR ON MY FACE, BECAUSE...

HEY IMPSTERS! LET'S PRACTICE THAT ELUSIVE FOURTH OBJECT!

•WHEW!•

I CAN JUGGLE THREE ITEMS REALLY WELL, BUT WHENEVER KIT TOSSED IN A FOURTH...

RRRRGH!

DON'T WORRY, YOU'VE STILL GOT A FEW YEARS BEFORE WE TAKE OUR JUGGLING SHOW ON THE ROAD.

THEN IT WAS TIME FOR MY FAVORITE PART OF FAIRE GET-TOGETHERS.

EVERYONE HAVE A TASTY BEVERAGE?

FELIX, HAND OVER THE DICE PLEASE.

CAN I PLAY, DAD?

I DUNNO, IMPY. DON'T YOU HAVE SCHOOL TOMORROW? AREN'T YOU SUPPOSED TO, LIKE, GO TO BED EARLY OR SOMETHING?

OOOO, LOOK AT YOU, BEING A RESPONSIBLE PARENT!

SO I SETTLED ON THE COUCH WITH FELIX INSTEAD. THAT'S ACTUALLY JUST AS FUN AS PLAYING MYSELF. IF YOU'VE NEVER PLAYED A ROLE-PLAYING GAME, IT'S BASICALLY A BIG GAME OF MAKE-BELIEVE. SINCE ALMOST EVERYONE HERE IS AN ACTOR, IT'S LIKE WATCHING A BIG, EXCITING ADVENTURE MOVIE. BUT BETTER.

SO OUR TROUPE OF MERRY MISCREANTS ARE ABOUT TO SET OUT ON THEIR VOYAGE THROUGH THE DEEP, DARK FOREST...

EVEN THOUGH I'M NOT PLAYING, I IMAGINE I'M AN ELF TAGGING ALONG ON THEIR ADVENTURE. IN THE GAME, I'M QUICK, CUNNING, AND BRAVE, AND THE VOYAGE INTO THE UNKNOWN DOESN'T SCARE ME.

I'M INVINCIBLE.

CHAPTER THREE

YE OLDE
MIDDLE SCHOOL

After months of preparations, including but not limited to careful outfit selection and triple-checking of school supplies, young Imogene is ready to embark on her journey into the Great Unknown. Like all explorers before her, our heroine has only one thought on her mind...

I CAN'T DO THIS!

I GUESS DAD CARRIED ME BACK TO MY ROOM LAST NIGHT. MAYBE IF I STAY QUIET, NO ONE WILL REMEMBER I'M SUPPOSED TO...

IMOGENE? TIME TO WAKE UP!

RATS!

OH IMPY, WHAT AN ADVENTURE! YOU ALWAYS AMAZE ME WITH HOW BRAVE YOU ARE.

I'M NOT BRAVE. I'M **TERRIFIED**.

I FELT LIKE I WAS GOING TO THROW UP AS I GOT DRESSED.

IT LOOKS LIKE EVERYONE SPENT THE NIGHT LAST NIGHT.

UMM...I'M LEAVING NOW. BYE.

ADIOS, MUCHACHA! ADIOS, MUUUUUUCHACHA!

FELIX, FELIX! MY HEAD! NOT SO LOUD!

OUR SCHOLAR! WE ARE SO PROUD OF YOU! HANG ON, LET ME TAKE A PICTURE.

CLICK!

DO YOU WANT US TO COME WITH YOU TO THE BUS STOP?

NOOOOO... THAT'S OK.

I DON'T WANT HER TO GOOOOOOOOO! **WAAAAAAAAAAA!**

OH HONEY, SHE'LL BE HOME SOON!

ALL OF A SUDDEN, I FELT LIKE I WAS GOING TO CRY. I WISH I COULD JUST STAY HOME AND EAT WAFFLES. I'D EVEN MISS FELIX.

YOU'D BETTER GO BEFORE THINGS GET COMPLETELY CRAZY AROUND HERE. REMEMBER, YOU'RE A KNIGHT-IN-TRAINING. CHIVALRY. HONESTY. BRAVERY. YOU GOT THIS.

WELL, HERE GOES NOTHING...

FROM WHAT EVERYONE TOLD ME LAST NIGHT, THE BUS WAS A HOT SPOT FOR BULLYING. BUT THE RIDE TO SCHOOL WAS SURPRISINGLY QUIET.

I MEAN "QUIET" IN THE "NOBODY BOTHERED ME" SORT OF WAY. NOT IN THE "QUIET" SORT OF WAY.

THEN WE PULLED UP TO SCHOOL.

I FELT STRANGELY OUTSIDE MY OWN BODY, LIKE I WAS WATCHING MYSELF ON TV. I COULDN'T BELIEVE I WAS **ACTUALLY** HERE. AT **MIDDLE SCHOOL**.

I **THOUGHT** I KNEW WHERE TO GO FROM THE ORIENTATION WE WENT TO A FEW WEEKS AGO...

BUT EVERYTHING LOOKED REALLY DIFFERENT WITH SO MANY KIDS AROUND.

EXCUSE ME, ARE YOU A TEACHER?

HAH, YEAH, I'M A TEACHER! YOU HAVE DETENTION FOR BOTHERING ME!

WHAT?!

OH MY GOD, JEREMY. YOU ARE SO MEAN!

GET TO CLASS, MR. CARR.

YOUNG LADY, ARE YOU LOST? THIS IS THE EIGHTH-GRADE WING—I'M GUESSING YOU'RE LOOKING FOR SIXTH.

HOW DID SHE KNOW?

ONCE I WAS IN THE RIGHT WING, I FOUND MY LOCKER AND OPENED IT WITH NO PROBLEM.

...ON THE FIFTH TRY.

I FOUND MY FIRST-PERIOD CLASSROOM AND MADE IT ON TIME.

I PICKED MY SEAT.

NOT FAR ENOUGH BACK TO BE A "BAD" KID, NOT CLOSE ENOUGH TO THE FRONT TO BE A TEACHER'S PET.

I SORT OF FELT LIKE A GHOST ALL MORNING AS I FLOATED FROM CLASS TO CLASS. ALL THE OTHER KIDS SEEMED TO KNOW EACH OTHER ALREADY. NOBODY SAID A WORD TO ME.

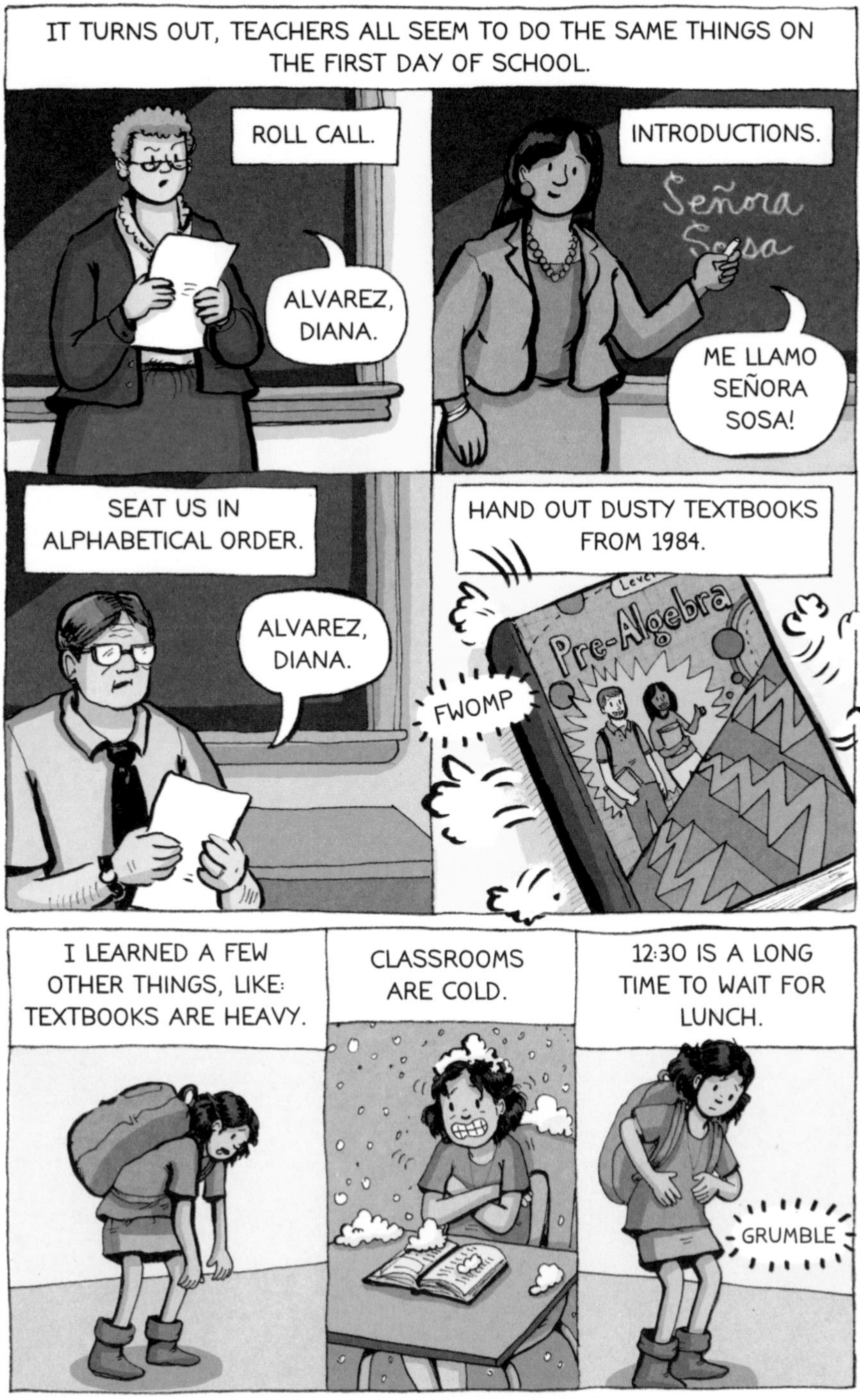
IT TURNS OUT, TEACHERS ALL SEEM TO DO THE SAME THINGS ON THE FIRST DAY OF SCHOOL.
ROLL CALL.
ALVAREZ, DIANA.
INTRODUCTIONS.
Señora Sosa
ME LLAMO SEÑORA SOSA!
SEAT US IN ALPHABETICAL ORDER.
ALVAREZ, DIANA.
HAND OUT DUSTY TEXTBOOKS FROM 1984.
Pre-Algebra
FWOMP
I LEARNED A FEW OTHER THINGS, LIKE: TEXTBOOKS ARE HEAVY.
CLASSROOMS ARE COLD.
12:30 IS A LONG TIME TO WAIT FOR LUNCH.
GRUMBLE

BY FOURTH PERIOD, I KIND OF HAD THINGS WORKED OUT.

ROOM 213... 213...

OH, FIE!

THIS TIME I HAD TO CHOOSE SOMEONE TO SIT WITH!

I DECIDED ON A GIRL I RECOGNIZED FROM MY SPANISH CLASS.

UM, HI. CAN I SIT HERE?

UMMM... OK.

OOOH, CUTE BOOTS. WHERE'D YOU GET THEM?

OH! ACTUALLY, SOMEBODY MADE THEM FOR ME.

CUSTOM BOOTS— THAT'S COOL.

OH HEY! EMILY! SIT HERE, SIT HERE!

IS THAT OK? SHE'S MY **BEST** FRIEND.

OH...OK.

THANK YOU SOOOOOO MUCH. YOU'RE **SOOO** NICE.

EEEEEEEE!

IF I'M **SOOOOO** NICE, WHY DIDN'T SHE WANT TO SIT WITH ME?

SIT

OOOH, JASON, WHO'S YOUR GIRLFRIEND?

GIRLFRIEND? I DON'T EVEN **KNOW** HER!

YEAH! WHO ARE YOU? WHERE'D YOU GO TO ELEMENTARY SCHOOL?

UM, I DIDN'T. I WAS HOMESCHOOLED.

IS THAT EVEN LEGAL?

WHAT'S 4 + 4?

DO YOU KNOW HOW TO READ?

YES, I KNOW HOW TO READ. I CAN SPELL TOO. TRY THIS ONE: I-D-I-O-T.

OOOOOOOO! HA-HA! SCORE ONE FOR HOMESCHOOL!

GENTLEMAN IN THE BLUE SHIRT AND YOUNG LADY IN THE PURPLE SHIRT. IF YOU ARE DONE FLIRTING WITH EACH OTHER...

OOOOOO! •GIGGLE GIGGLE•

...WE CAN GET STARTED. IF YOU CAN ALL KEEP YOUR RAGING HORMONES IN CHECK, WE MAY JUST BE ABLE TO DO SOME SCIENCE THIS YEAR.

MY NAME IS **DOCTOR** MACGREGOR. NOT **MISTER** MACGREGOR. I DID NOT GO TO SCHOOL FOR EIGHT YEARS TO BE CALLED **MISTER** MACGREGOR.

YOU IN THE FRONT ROW. WHAT IS YOUR NAME?

ANITA.

ANITA, TAKE THESE TEXTBOOKS AND PASS THEM BACK.

SCIENCE CLASS PRETTY MUCH WENT LIKE THE OTHERS...EXCEPT **DOCTOR** MACGREGOR SEEMED WAY MORE STRICT THAN MY OTHER TEACHERS.

WE WILL HAVE A TEST EVERY WEEK IN THIS CLASS. IF YOU RECEIVE A GRADE LESS THAN A C, YOU WILL NEED TO HAVE IT SIGNED BY AN ADULT.

BRRRIIING!

THIS IS NOW SIXTH-GRADE LUNCH, SO EXIT THE CLASSROOM **QUIETLY** AND PROCEED TO THE MULTI-PURPOSE ROOM.

JASON AND HOMESCHOOL, SITTING IN A TREE! K-I-S-S-I...

LIKE I SAID, I KNOW HOW TO SPELL—I KNEW WHAT CAME NEXT.

AS IF THAT WASN'T BAD ENOUGH, NOW CAME THE PART OF THE DAY I'D BEEN DREADING THE MOST...

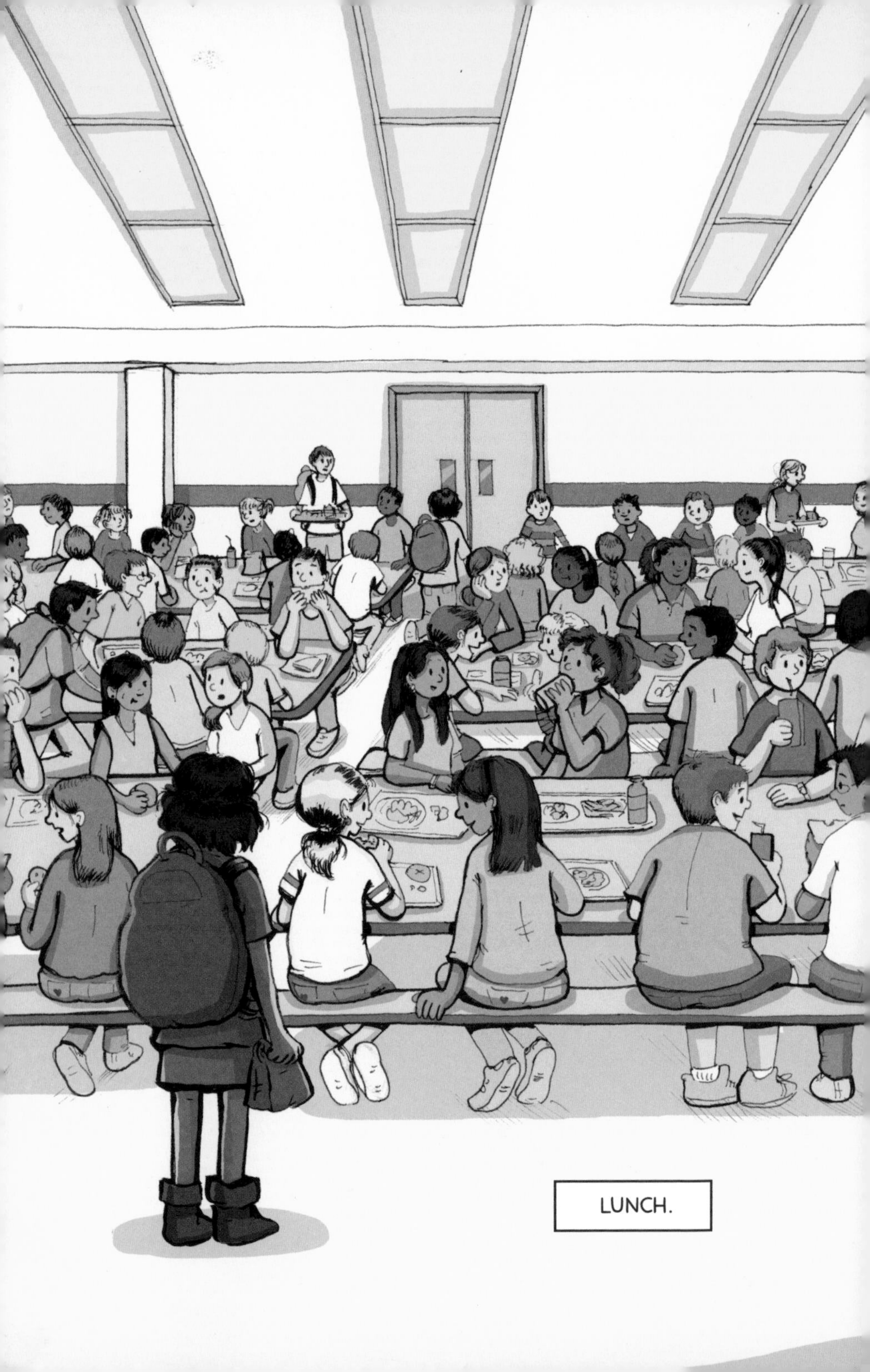
LUNCH.

WHO WAS I SUPPOSED TO SIT WITH? ALL OF MY WORST NIGHTMARES WERE COMING TRUE.

THIS WAS WORSE THAN BEING TRAPPED IN A DEEP PIT, BEING CLAWED AT BY TROLLS AND EARTHWORMS...

IMOGENE?

YOUR NAME IS IMOGENE, RIGHT? FROM SCIENCE CLASS? COME SIT WITH US!

SCOOCH

I THINK ONE OF THE NICEST FEELINGS IN THE WORLD HAS TO BE SOMEONE SCOOCHING OVER FOR YOU.

I'M MIKA, AND THAT'S SASHA AND EMILY.

I FIGURED YOU DIDN'T KNOW ANYONE, SINCE YOU WERE HOMESCHOOLED.

YOU WERE **HOMESCHOOLED**? ARE YOUR PARENTS, LIKE, SUPER-RELIGIOUS OR SOMETHING?

NOOO...THEY HOMESCHOOLED US BECAUSE... BECAUSE...

...THEY DIDN'T AGREE WITH THE STATE CURRICULUM, HEH-HEH.

OH. BORING.

I FIGURED I'D WAIT UNTIL I KNEW THEM LONGER THAN 8.3 SECONDS TO TELL THEM MY FAMILY WORKED AT THE RENAISSANCE FAIRE. THAT INFORMATION WAS NOT FOR THE FAINT OF HEART.

JASON! IT'S YOUR GIRRRRLFRIEND! DON'T YOU WANT TO SHARE YOUR FRENCH FRIES WITH HER OR SOMETHING?

SHUT UP. THE FIRST THING YOU NEED TO KNOW, IMOGENE, IS THAT THOSE BOYS ARE IDIOTS. DON'T PAY ANY ATTENTION TO THEM.

IDIOTS. GOT IT.

I FINALLY RELAXED A LITTLE BIT AS EVERYONE STARTED LAUGHING AND TALKING AROUND ME. WAS IT POSSIBLE? WAS I REALLY MAKING...**FRIENDS**?!?

THE REST OF THE DAY PASSED PRETTY QUICKLY.
I HAD THREE PERIODS AFTER LUNCH.

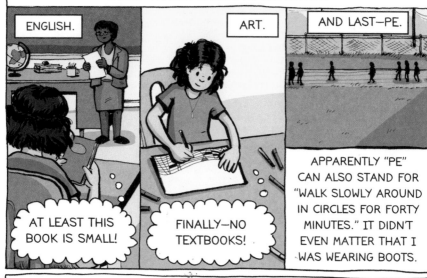

ENGLISH.

ART.

AND LAST—PE.

AT LEAST THIS BOOK IS SMALL!

FINALLY—NO TEXTBOOKS!

APPARENTLY "PE" CAN ALSO STAND FOR "WALK SLOWLY AROUND IN CIRCLES FOR FORTY MINUTES." IT DIDN'T EVEN MATTER THAT I WAS WEARING BOOTS.

YOU KNOW HOW SOME DAYS PASS AND NOTHING NEW OR EXCITING HAPPENS...BUT THEN ON **SOME** DAYS SO MANY THINGS HAPPEN, YOU CAN'T BELIEVE IT WAS ALL ONE DAY?

SEE YOU TOMORROW, IMOGENE!

OH YEAH—I HAVE TO DO THIS ALL OVER AGAIN **TOMORROW**!

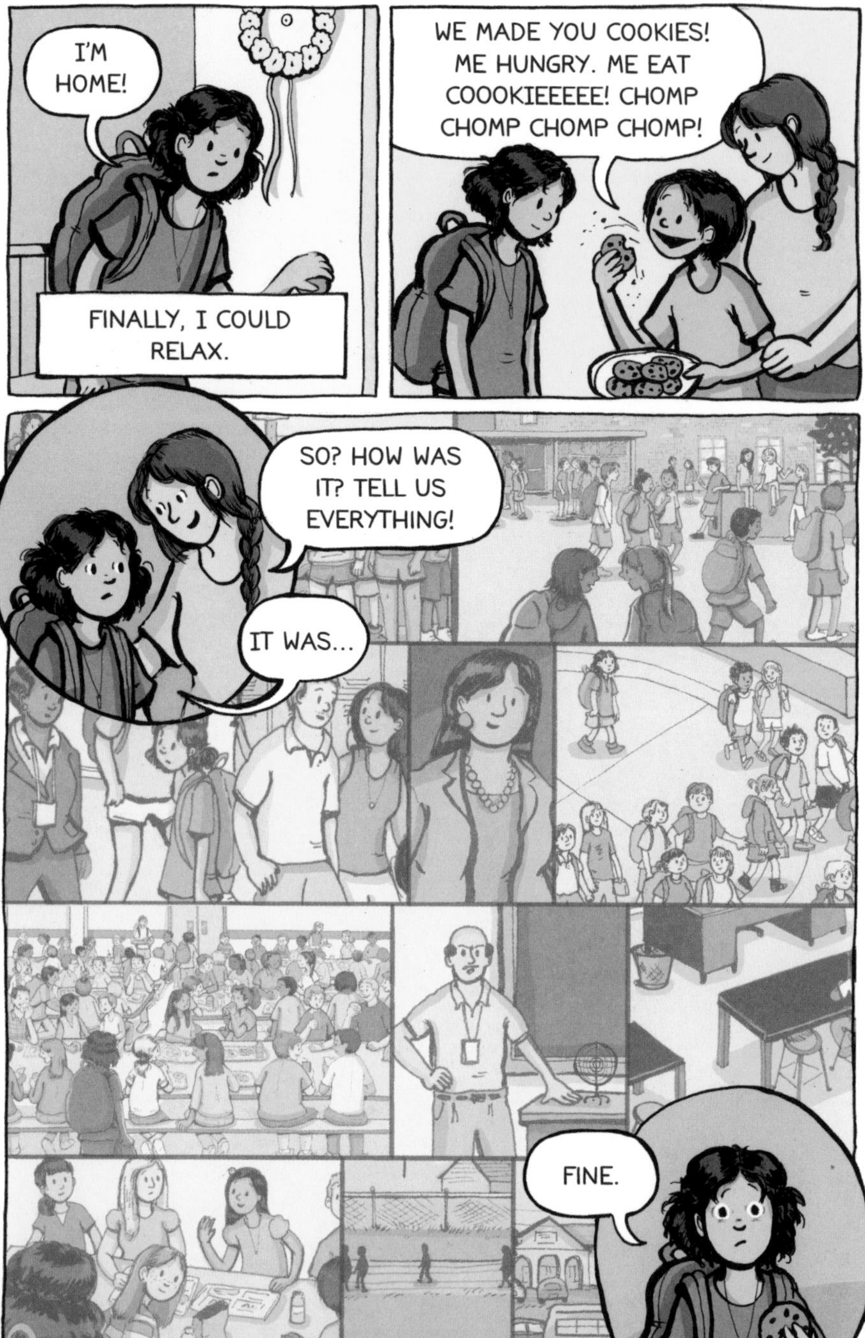
I'M HOME!
FINALLY, I COULD RELAX.
WE MADE YOU COOKIES! ME HUNGRY. ME EAT COOOKIEEEEE! CHOMP CHOMP CHOMP CHOMP!
SO? HOW WAS IT? TELL US EVERYTHING!
IT WAS...
FINE.

THE REST OF THE WEEK WAS PRETTY GOOD. MIKA AND HER FRIENDS WERE NICE. SHE EVEN INVITED ME TO HER BIRTHDAY PARTY IN A FEW WEEKS!

UH-HUH!

I'M INVITED TO A PARTY!

MY MOM HAS TO GET THE INVITATIONS PRINTED. BUT **FIRST** I HAVE TO DECIDE WHERE I WANT TO HAVE IT. I THOUGHT MAYBE THE WATER PARK, BUT THAT'S WHERE I HAD MY PARTY **LAST** YEAR, SO...

JASON AND HIS FRIENDS WERE **VERY** ANNOYING, BUT KIND OF FUNNY, TOO.

NOBODY HAD PICKED ON ME...YET.

NOTE TO SELF: NO ROLLY BACKPACKS.

MOST OF MY TEACHERS WERE OK, EXCEPT FOR A CERTAIN YOU-KNOW-WHO.

THIS LAB BOOK HAS SUCH ATROCIOUS HANDWRITING, I CANNOT EVEN READ IT.

HEY!

57

IN FACT, MY FIRST WEEK KINDA FLEW BY. BEFORE I KNEW IT, IT WAS FRIDAY. AND THAT MEANT...

DRESS REHEARSAL DAY!

MY FIRST DAY AS A SQUIRE WAS NOT EXACTLY THE BEST DAY OF MY LIFE, BUT DRESS REHEARSAL DAY WAS STILL EXCITING. EVERY YEAR MY MOM SEWS EVERYONE IN THE FAMILY A NEW COSTUME. IT'S TRADITION THAT WE DON'T GET TO SEE THEM UNTIL DRESS REHEARSAL DAY.

CAN WE OPEN THEM NOW?

MMMHMMM. GO WAKE YOUR BROTHER.

MORNINGS ARE NOT FELIX'S FAVORITE TIME OF DAY. WAKING HIM UP REQUIRES A GENTLE TOUCH.

Felix Keep Out

WAKE UP!!!

DONE!

LAST YEAR FELIX WENT FIRST, SO IMPY, IT'S YOUR TURN.

YIPPEEE!

OH! I LOVE IT!!!

MY TUNIC HAD THE FAMILY CREST ON THE FRONT—THAT HELPED IDENTIFY WHICH KNIGHT I WAS A SQUIRE FOR.

MY TURN! MY TURN!

UNZIP

IT'S...

THE SAME!

LISTEN, FELIX HAS BEEN A BIT JEALOUS WITH ALL THE ATTENTION YOU'RE GETTING OVER BEING A SQUIRE, AND GOING TO SCHOOL. YOU KNOW THAT HE WANTS TO BE JUST LIKE YOU, AND I THOUGHT HAVING A MATCHING COSTUME MIGHT MAKE HIM FEEL BETTER.

I GUESS IT WAS NICE THAT FELIX WANTED TO BE LIKE ME. BUT DID OUR COSTUMES HAVE TO LOOK **EXACTLY** THE SAME?

NOW WE ARE **TWINS**, IMPY!!

AND THIS IS YOUR DAD'S TUNIC, AND MY NEW BODICE! NOW THE WHOLE FAMILY WILL BE SUPPORTING OUR KNIGHT AND OUR SQUIRE!

IMPS? WHAT DO YOU SAY TO YOUR MOM? SHE WAS UP REALLY LATE LAST NIGHT FINISHING THESE UP.

THANKS, MOM. THEY'RE GREAT. I REALLY LOVE THEM.

I'D BETTER GET READY FOR SCHOOL.

MY MOM ONCE MADE US WATCH THIS CRAZY SHOW THAT WAS APPARENTLY THE "COOL HIP THING" ONCE UPON A TIME. FOR SOME REASON, THE MATCHING FAMILY OUTFITS MADE ME THINK OF THAT NOW...

SCHOOL WAS...SCHOOL. I WASN'T AS NERVOUS AS I'D BEEN THE FIRST DAY, BUT I WASN'T EXACTLY COMFORTABLE EITHER.

MIKA AND HER FRIENDS WERE NICE, BUT SOMETIMES I DIDN'T KNOW WHAT TO SAY TO THEM. I WAS AFRAID OF SAYING SOMETHING STUPID, THAT WOULD MAKE THEM REALIZE I WAS A NERD AND THEY SHOULDN'T BE HANGING OUT WITH ME.

EARTH TO IMOGENE! I **SAID**, WHAT'S YOUR FAVORITE STORE AT THE MALL?

HMMM? OH, UH... THE...PRETZEL PLACE?

OH MY GOD, IMOGENE, YOU ARE **SO** FUNNY. YOU'RE A NATIONAL TREASURE, YOU KNOW THAT?

HA-HA... HA?

I WAS SO GLAD MY FIRST WEEK WAS OVER. FINALLY IT WAS THE WEEKEND. I DIDN'T HAVE TO WORRY ABOUT SCHOOL...OR TEACHERS...OR FRIENDS...

IS THAT YOUR CAR? THE RUSTY ONE?

UM, YEAH. SEE YOU MONDAY!

I GUESS OUR CAR **IS** KIND OF OLD.

61

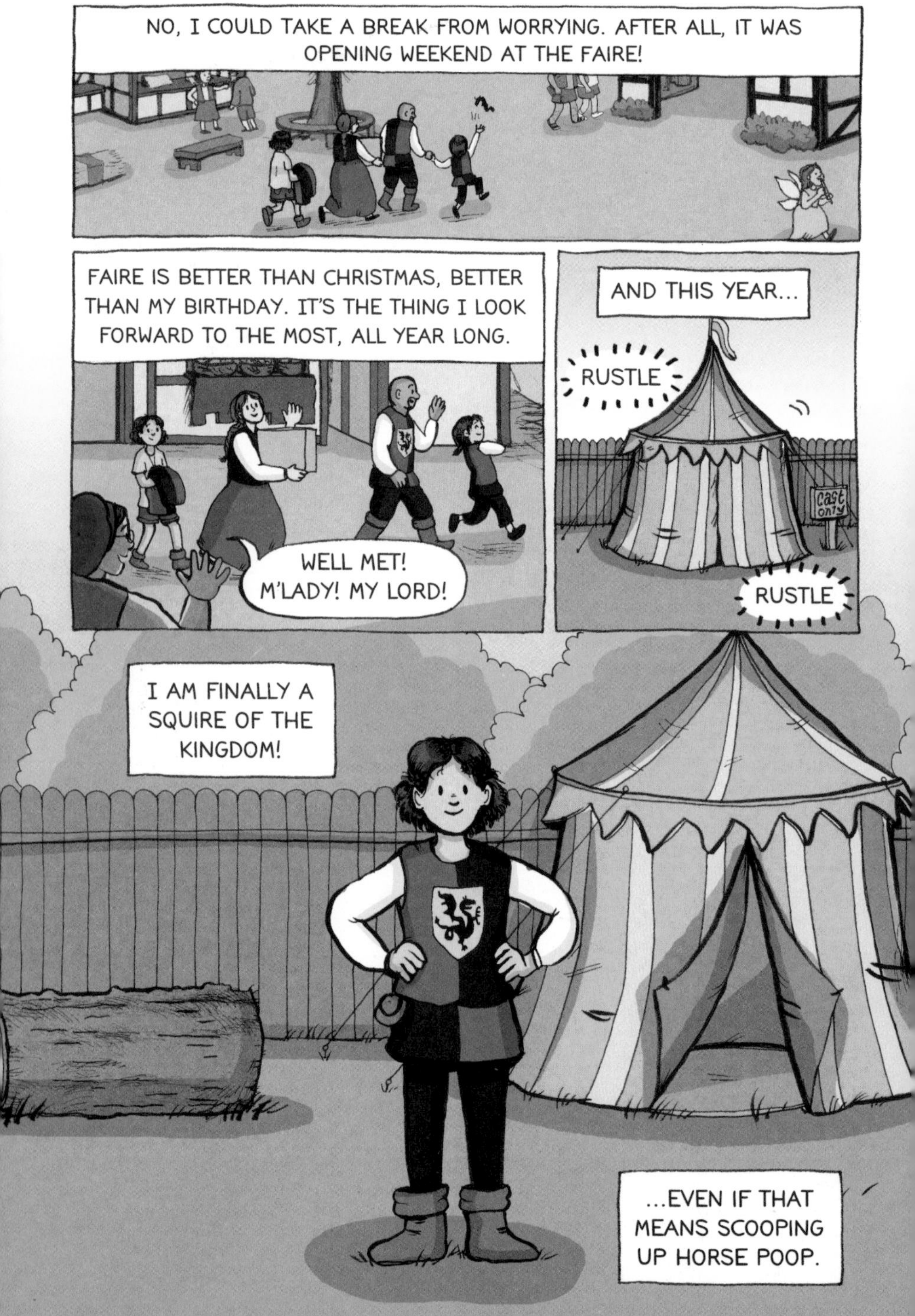
NO, I COULD TAKE A BREAK FROM WORRYING. AFTER ALL, IT WAS OPENING WEEKEND AT THE FAIRE!
FAIRE IS BETTER THAN CHRISTMAS, BETTER THAN MY BIRTHDAY. IT'S THE THING I LOOK FORWARD TO THE MOST, ALL YEAR LONG.
WELL MET! M'LADY! MY LORD!
AND THIS YEAR...
RUSTLE
CAST ONLY
RUSTLE
I AM FINALLY A SQUIRE OF THE KINGDOM!
...EVEN IF THAT MEANS SCOOPING UP HORSE POOP.

DURING THE DRESS REHEARSAL, WE RAN THROUGH THE BIG EVENTS: THE JOUST AND THE HUMAN CHESS MATCH.

I DON'T GET TO DO MUCH IN THE CHESS MATCH—I'M ONLY A PAWN FOR MY DAD'S SIDE—BUT AT LEAST I GET A FRONT-ROW SEAT TO ALL THE BATTLES.

THE NIGHT BEFORE OPENING DAY, THERE'S ALWAYS A BIG PARTY BACKSTAGE—BACK WHERE THE CAMPGROUND IS.

THERE'S SINGING, BELLY DANCING, JUGGLING, AND THE MOST DELICIOUS FOOD YOU CAN IMAGINE.

EVEN FELIX WASN'T AS ANNOYING AS USUAL.

CAN I COME UP?

I WAS FILLED WITH CHEER AND GOODWILL, SO...

SURE.

I WAS A **LITTLE** NERVOUS ABOUT MY FIRST DAY AS A SQUIRE...BUT IT WAS NOTHING COMPARED TO THE FIRST DAY OF MIDDLE SCHOOL.

AT LEAST I KNEW I BELONGED **HERE**.

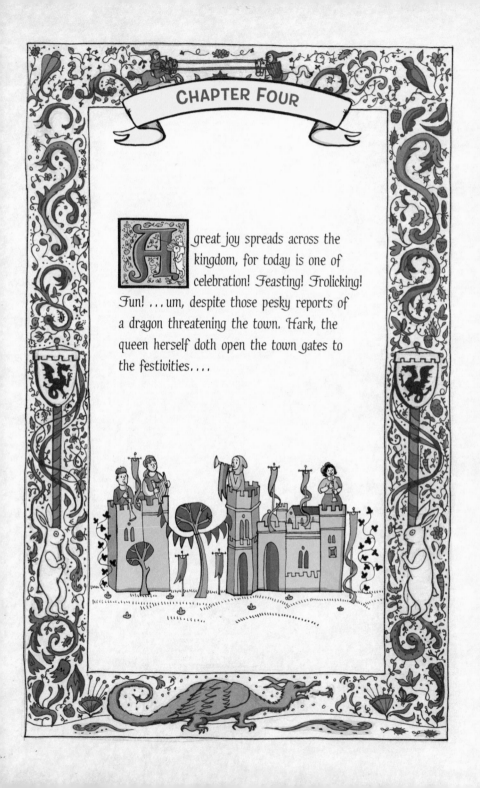

CHAPTER FOUR

great joy spreads across the kingdom, for today is one of celebration! Feasting! Frolicking! Fun! ...um, despite those pesky reports of a dragon threatening the town. Hark, the queen herself doth open the town gates to the festivities....

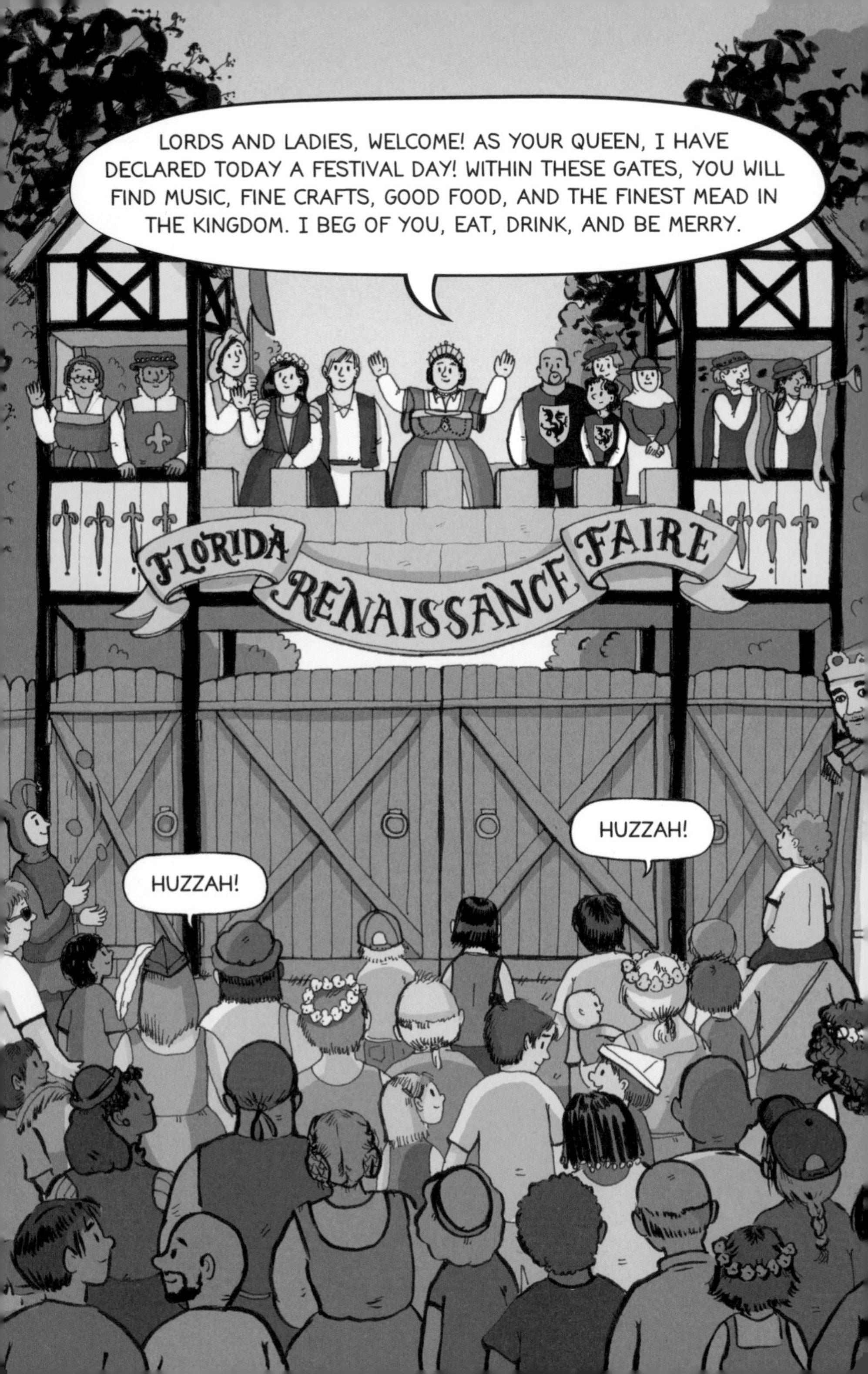
LORDS AND LADIES, WELCOME! AS YOUR QUEEN, I HAVE DECLARED TODAY A FESTIVAL DAY! WITHIN THESE GATES, YOU WILL FIND MUSIC, FINE CRAFTS, GOOD FOOD, AND THE FINEST MEAD IN THE KINGDOM. I BEG OF YOU, EAT, DRINK, AND BE MERRY.
FLORIDA RENAISSANCE FAIRE
HUZZAH!
HUZZAH!

FEELING NERVOUS?

MMMM...JUST A LITTLE.

YOUR MAJESTY! YOUR MAJESTY!

YES, HERMIT? WHAT IS IT?

YOUR MAJESTY, I BEG OF YOU, **DO NOT OPEN THESE GATES**! I HAVE EMERGED FROM MY CAVE FOR THE FIRST TIME IN FORTY-SEVEN YEARS AND...OH MY. FASHIONS SEEM TO HAVE CHANGED.

WHERE WAS I...OH YES. YOUR MAJESTY, I BRING TIDINGS OF GREAT DANGER FOR THIS VILLAGE AND ALL OF THESE FINE CITIZENS! THEIR VERY **LIVES** DEPEND ON IT!

AND WHAT IS THIS "GREAT DANGER" OF WHICH YOU SPEAK?

IT IS... A **DRAGON**.

GOOD HEAVENS, HERMIT, YOU GAVE ME A FRIGHT. EVERYONE KNOWS THERE ARE NO SUCH THINGS AS **DRAGONS**.

NO SUCH THING AS DRAGONS?! BUT...I SEE FAIRIES OVER THERE, AND OGRES, AND...I DON'T KNOW **WHAT** THAT GUY IS.

HA!

HA!

HERMIT, YOU TRULY ARE A FOOL. DO NOT YE KNOW THAT THE BRAVEST KNIGHTS IN ALL THE LAND SERVE AS MY PROTECTORS? SIR GEORGE, WHAT SAY YOU TO THIS DRAGON BUSINESS?

YOUR MAJESTY, IF ANY CREATURE THREATENS THIS KINGDOM—HAVE NO FEAR BUT I SHALL SMITE IT!

YOUR MAJESTY, I TOO PLEDGE MY SERVICE TO YOUR HIGHNESS! MY LOYAL SQUIRE AND I GIVE YOU OUR WORD OF HONOR.

DON'T TRUST SIR HUGO, M'LADY! WEREN'T HE **BANISHED** FROM THE KINGDOM FOR DEALIN' IN...IN...DRAGONS?

DRAGONS, POPPYCOCK. ENOUGH. WE SHALL DELAY THIS FESTIVAL NO LONGER. GOOD CITIZENS, WELCOME TO THIS FAIR CITY, AND FEAR NOT. ENTER, AND BE MERRY. HUZZAH!

WELL DONE, IMPY! YOUR FIRST PROFESSIONAL ACTING GIG, IN THE BAG. TIME TO DO SOME WELCOMING DUTIES—LET'S GO!

OUR NEXT JOB WAS TO HELP WELCOME VISITORS TO THE FAIRE. I DIDN'T REALLY KNOW WHAT TO SAY, SO I JUST HUNG AROUND MY DAD AND LISTENED.

I HEAR THIS DRAGON IS POISONING THE VERY RIVERS AND STREAMS OF THIS TOWN. THIS IS VERY IMPORTANT—YOU **MUST NOT** BATHE IN THE STREAM. I KNOW YOU PROBABLY HAVE NOT BATHED IN SIX-ODD MONTHS, BUT STILL.

HA!

HA!

I SAY, DON'T WORRY ABOUT THIS "DRAGON" BUSINESS. THEY ARE VERY MISUNDERSTOOD ANIMALS, LIKE PIT BULLS.

HA!

HA!

BEWARE, GENTLE FOLK! DO NOT BE FOOLED BY SIR HUGO'S DASHING GOOD LOOKS!

I SAY, DO I **LOOK** LIKE A BAD GUY?

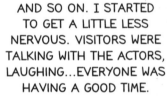

...I **SAID**, DO I **LOOK** LIKE A BAD GUY?

OH. SORRY, M'LORD.

THIS WAS ONE OF OUR RUNNING GAGS. WHENEVER MY DAD SAID, "DO I LOOK LIKE A BAD GUY?" I WAS SUPPOSED TO RUN BEHIND HIM AND BILLOW OUT HIS CAPE AS HE GAVE AN EVIL LAUGH.

BWA-HA-HA-HA-HAAAAAA!

AND SO ON. I STARTED TO GET A LITTLE LESS NERVOUS. VISITORS WERE TALKING WITH THE ACTORS, LAUGHING...EVERYONE WAS HAVING A GOOD TIME.

ATTEND, SQUIRE. I MUST AWAY TO THE ROYAL COURT. I EXPECT YOU TO MINGLE WITH THESE PEASANTS...ER, I MEAN, THESE FINE AND NOBLE CITIZENS, UNTIL THE ROYAL PROCESSION.

IN PLAIN ENGLISH, THAT MEANT...I WAS ON MY OWN FOR THE NEXT HOUR.

GULP.

IT WASN'T SO EASY STRIKING UP CONVERSATIONS WITH RANDOM STRANGERS WHEN I WAS DOING STREET ALL ALONE.

EVERYONE ELSE SEEMED TO KNOW WHAT THEY WERE DOING. THE WELL WENCHES WERE WENCHING IT UP. THE MUD PIT PLAYERS WERE FLINGING MUD.

THE MINSTRELS, THE JUGGLERS, THE SHOPKEEPERS...EVERYONE HAD SOMETHING TO DO. EXCEPT ME.

SO, I DID WHAT I DO BEST.

OI! GIRL! THERE IS ONLY **ONE** HERMIT IN THIS SHIRE, AND THAT'S ME!

TUG

HEH-HEH, HI, CUSSIE.

ARE YE BILKIN' HER ROYAL HIGHNESS FOR TWENTY POUNDS A WEEK BY SITTIN' IN A TREE ALL DAY?

I DON'T KNOW WHAT TO **SAY** TO PEOPLE.

REMEMBER, YOU'RE NOT REALLY **YOU**; YOU'RE PLAYIN' A CHARACTER. DO YOU THINK I AM NATURALLY THIS CHARISMATIC AND BEAUTIFUL IN REAL LIFE?

WHAT ARE YOU LAUGHIN' AT, YOU FROTHY HEDGE-BORN FLIRT-GILL?

BUT WHAT DO I **DO**?

YOU DO **ANYTHING**! THAT IS THE JOY OF THE RENAISSANCE FAIRE! YOU CAN DO AND SAY ANYTHING YE WANT AND NOT GET IN TROUBLE FOR IT HERE!

WATCH THIS.

YOU SIR! YOU MUST BE A BRAVE AND NOBLE KNIGHT, TO HAVE SLAIN A DRAGON AND WEAR ITS PELT UPON YOUR CHEST! WILST THOU PROTECT A FAIR AND VIRTUOUS MAIDEN FROM ANY DRAGONS HEREABOUTS?

AYE, I SHALL! LET ME KNOW IF YOU SEE ANY VIRTUOUS MAIDENS AROUND!

SMACK

OH! YOU WICKED, WICKED MAN!

YOU SEE, IMOGENE? YOU SAY ANYTHING YOU WANT!

YOU SIR! IS IT TRUE WHAT THEY SAY ABOUT A SCOT AND HIS KILT?

SHE MAKES IT LOOK SO EASY. I'M JUST NOT AS BRAVE AS SHE IS.

SOMETIMES WHEN YOU'RE IN AN UNCOMFORTABLE SITUATION,

AVOIDANCE IS THE WAY TO GO.

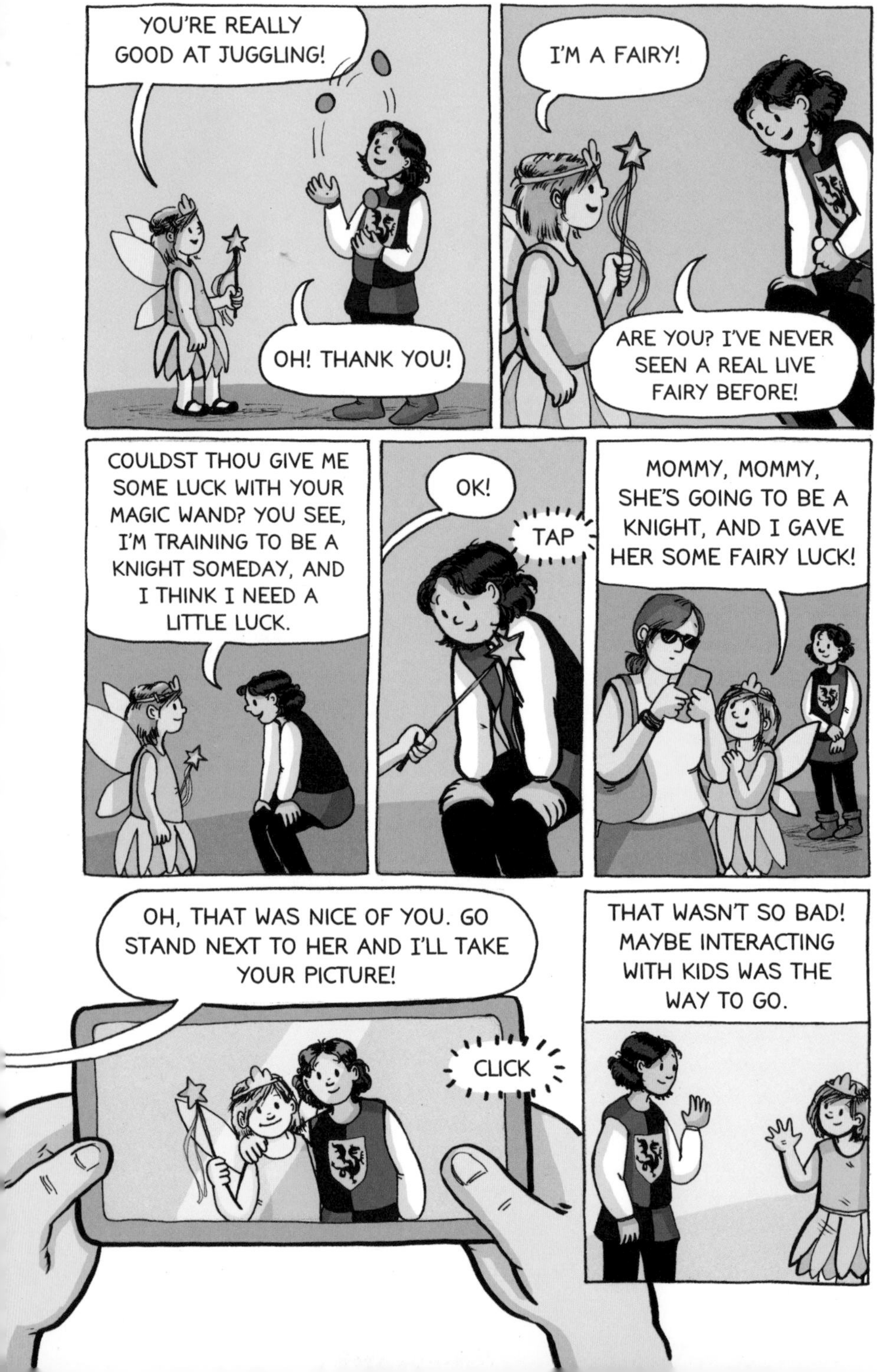
YOU'RE REALLY GOOD AT JUGGLING!
OH! THANK YOU!
I'M A FAIRY!
ARE YOU? I'VE NEVER SEEN A REAL LIVE FAIRY BEFORE!
COULDST THOU GIVE ME SOME LUCK WITH YOUR MAGIC WAND? YOU SEE, I'M TRAINING TO BE A KNIGHT SOMEDAY, AND I THINK I NEED A LITTLE LUCK.
OK!
TAP
MOMMY, MOMMY, SHE'S GOING TO BE A KNIGHT, AND I GAVE HER SOME FAIRY LUCK!
OH, THAT WAS NICE OF YOU. GO STAND NEXT TO HER AND I'LL TAKE YOUR PICTURE!
CLICK
THAT WASN'T SO BAD! MAYBE INTERACTING WITH KIDS WAS THE WAY TO GO.

FOR SOME REASON, JUGGLING MADE IT EASIER TO TALK TO PEOPLE.

GOOD KNIGHT, I AM AT YOUR SERVICE.

HEE-HEE!

'TIS NOT MAGIC, I ASSURE YOU! JUST LOTS OF PRACTICE!

SO EMBOLDENED, I DECIDED TO TALK TO SOMEONE MY **OWN** SIZE.

GOOD DAY, M'LADY. YOU MUST BE A VISITING DIGNITARY OF SOME SORT WITH SUCH FINE ATTIRE.

HELLO, IMOGENE.

OH! UH...

HOW DO YOU KNOW MY NAME? YOU LOOK REALLY FAMILIAR...

WE GO TO THE SAME SCHOOL.

OH.

OHHHHHH!

ANITA, RIGHT? YOU'RE...IN MY SCIENCE CLASS.

AND YOUR SPANISH AND GYM CLASSES.

I FELT A LITTLE DUMB FOR NOT KNOWING THAT.

DO YOU WORK HERE TOO? I THOUGHT I KNEW ALL THE CAST MEMBERS...

NAY. MY FATHER AND I HAVE SEASON TICKETS, SO WE DRESS UP AND COME EVERY WEEKEND.

SQUIRE! YOU ARE NOT BOTHERING THESE FINE AND IMPORTANT FOLK, ARE YOU?

GOOD SIR, SHE WAS NOT. WE ARE ACQUAINTANCES FROM SCHOOL.

AH! WELL, IF YOU ARE ACQUAINTANCES, I HOPE WE WILL HAVE YOUR SUPPORT THIS DAY AT THE JOUST. A ROSE FOR A ROSE, M'LADY.

IT WAS AMAZING. ANITA LOOKED SO DIFFERENT THAN SHE DID AT SCHOOL. SHE LOOKED REGAL AND...

HAPPY.

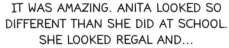

THE REST OF THE DAY FLEW BY, AND SOON IT WAS TIME FOR... THE JOUST! WHEN MOST PEOPLE THINK OF THE RENAISSANCE FAIRE, THEY THINK ABOUT TURKEY LEGS AND THE JOUST. IT **IS** ONE OF THE MOST EXCITING PARTS OF THE DAY.

THE ARENA WAS DIVIDED INTO TWO HALVES—THE GOLD SECTION FOR SIR GEORGE, AND THE BLACK SECTION FOR MY DAD. PART OF MY JOB WAS TO GET THE CROWD IN MY DAD'S SECTION EXCITED—NOT THAT THEY REALLY NEEDED MY HELP.

HIP-HIP...

HUZZAH!

GOOD PEOPLE, WE HAVE ALL ENJOYED A DAY OF FESTIVITY WITHOUT SIGHT OF THIS DREADED DRAGON. THEREFORE, LET US CELEBRATE AS THESE BRAVE KNIGHTS SHOW THEIR SKILL ON THE JOUSTING FIELD!

YOUR MAJESTY, MY STRENGTH AND SKILL IS IN SERVICE TO YOUR MAJESTY AND TO ALL OF ENGLAND.

I TOO PLEDGE MYSELF TO YOUR MAJESTY AND TO ENGLAND.

LIAR! MY QUEEN, THIS SIR HUGO IS A SCOUNDREL AND A KNAVE, AND MEANS TO CONQUER THIS FAIR CITY FOR HIS OWN PERSONAL GAIN!

WHAT?! I ASK YOU, FAIR CITIZENS: DO I **LOOK** LIKE A BAD GUY?

BWA-HA-HA-HA-HA!

FOR SUCH SLANDEROUS REMARKS, I CHALLENGE YOU, SIR GEORGE, TO A DUEL! SQUIRE, FETCH ME MY STEED AND MY LANCE!

THIS IS WHERE THE ACTION BEGINS!

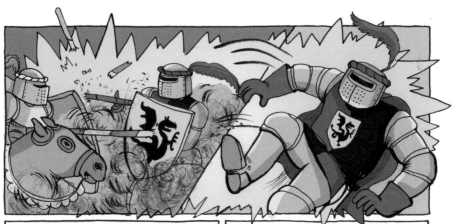

I SHALL SPARE YOUR LIFE, AS LONG AS YOU SWEAR TO LEAVE OUR CITY AND NEVER RETURN!

OH YES, I SWEAR IT. YOU'VE NOTHING TO FEAR HERE ANYMORE, NOTHING TO FEAR...

MY FAVORITE PART OF THE SHOW!

NOW, SQUIRE!

SAY YOUR PRAYERS, SIR GEORGE!

STOP, SIR HUGO! SPARE HIS LIFE, AND I WILL MARRY YOU AND YOU SHALL BE RULER OF THIS CITY!

MY DEAREST!

IT IS THE ONLY WAY!

WORKS FOR ME. GUARDS...KILL HIM ANYWAY.

YOU **SCOUNDREL**!

SHOVE

DID YOU REALLY THINK YOU COULD WIN, SIR HUGO?

YOU FOOL. ST. GEORGE AND THE DRAGON IS A WELL-KNOWN TALE—**EVERYONE** KNOWS HOW THIS ENDS! I DEFEAT THE EVIL DRAGON—GOOD **ALWAYS** TRIUMPHS OVER EVIL!

SIR GEORGE, WE THANK YOU FOR EXPOSING THE SCOUNDREL SIR HUGO, AND FOR PROTECTING THIS CITY. I WELCOME THEE TO A HERO'S PARADE THROUGHOUT THE CITY. THREE CHEERS FOR SIR GEORGE! HIP-HIP...

HUZZAH!

WELL PLAYED, IMPSTERS. COME ON, LET'S JOIN THE PARADE.

I WAS FRAMED! **YOU** BELIEVE ME, RIGHT?

THE AFTERNOON PARADE ENDS AT THE GATES FOR THE CLOSING CEREMONY.

AND NOW, GOOD CITIZENS, WE MUST CLOSE THE GATE FOR NIGHTLY CURFEW. WE WOULD NOT WANT EVIL MARAUDERS ATTACKING OUR CITY. WE BID YOU ADIEU.

THAT WAS QUITE IMPRESSIVE. I DIDN'T REALIZE CHILDREN COULD BE PART OF THE SHOWS. YOU WEREN'T IN THE SHOWS **LAST** YEAR.

OH. YEAH. LAST YEAR I WORKED AT MY MOM'S SHOPPE. IT'S PROBABLY WHERE YOU GOT THAT WREATH.

WELL, YOU'RE REALLY LUCKY TO SPEND ALL YOUR TIME HERE. MY DAD AND I LOOK FORWARD TO IT EACH YEAR.

I GUESS I'M LUCKY... ARE YOU COMING BACK TOMORROW?

I AM. I SHALL SEE YOU THEN. GOOD DAY, IMOGENE.

THE DAILY SCHEDULE AT THE FAIRE STAYS BASICALLY THE SAME, SO SUNDAY RAN JUST LIKE SATURDAY. I WAS MORE PREPARED FOR STREET PERFORMING ON DAY TWO.

CAN YOU TEACH ME HOW TO DO THAT?

OH. I GUESS SO!

ANNIE! WE'RE GOING TO GET SOME BEER. YOU STAY HERE.

OK, SO YOU START WITH TWO BAGS IN YOUR LEFT HAND AND ONE IN YOUR RIGHT...

BEFORE I KNEW IT, I HAD A WHOLE GANG OF KIDS SURROUNDING ME WANTING TO LEARN HOW TO JUGGLE.

WELL! LOOKS LIKE YE HAVE FOUND A WAY TO INTERACT WITH YOUR AUDIENCE, EH!

AYE, I SUPPOSE I HAVE!

MY STREET HOURS FLEW BY WITH MY NEW JUGGLING SCHOOL. IN THE AFTERNOON, ALL THE KIDS WERE SO OCCUPIED, I HAD TIME TO PRACTICE MY BLOCKING.

GOOD DAY, IMOGENE.

ANITA! GOOD DAY!

I SEE THOU ART WELL VERSED IN THE ART OF THE SWORD. I TOO KNOW A BIT OF SWORDPLAY.

YOU DO?

FOR SOME REASON, ANITA DIDN'T STRIKE ME AS A SWORDPLAY KIND OF GAL.

I TAKE FENCING. MOST IVY LEAGUES LIKE YOU TO PRACTICE SOME SORT OF SPORT.

YOU WANT TO BORROW A SWORD AND SPAR WITH ME?

NAY. I AM OFF TO VIEW A SPECTACLE WITH MY FATHER. BUT PERHAPS NEXT WEEKEND.

SO, SHE WAS A **LITTLE** WEIRD. BUT IT WAS REASSURING TO KNOW I'D HAVE AT LEAST **ONE** OTHER FRIEND AT SCHOOL TOMORROW.

NOT THAT I WAS ALREADY NERVOUS ABOUT SCHOOL OR ANYTHING.

TOTALLY NERVOUS

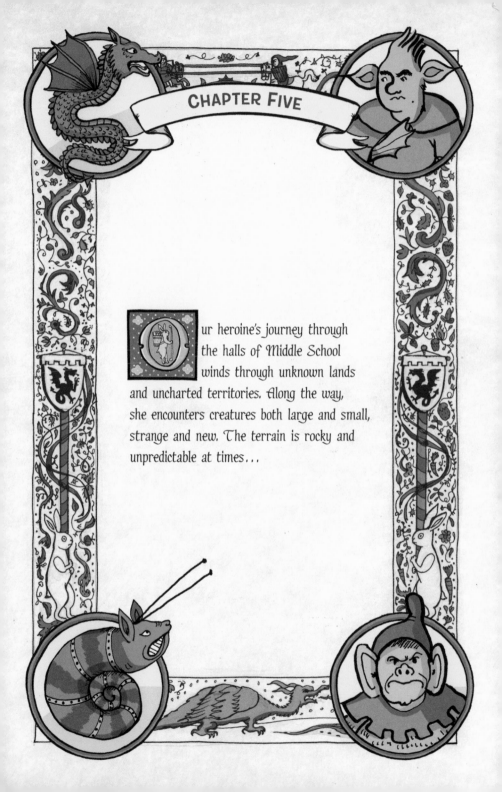

CHAPTER FIVE

Our heroine's journey through the halls of Middle School winds through unknown lands and uncharted territories. Along the way, she encounters creatures both large and small, strange and new. The terrain is rocky and unpredictable at times...

SO FAR, MIDDLE SCHOOL IS JUST...**WEIRD**. I'M STILL TRYING TO FIGURE OUT THE RULES, AND IT'S EXHAUSTING.

HEY ANITA! HOW'S IT GOING?

WE PROBABLY SHOULDN'T TALK TOO MUCH AT SCHOOL.

WHAT? WHY NOT?

JUST TRUST ME. IT WILL BE EASIER. YOU'LL THANK ME LATER.

?

ONCE YOU **DO** FIGURE OUT THE RULES, THEY CAN CHANGE WITHOUT WARNING.

HEY IMOGENE! HOW COME YOU WEAR THOSE BOOTS, LIKE, EVERY DAY?

MY BOOTS? I'M SUPPOSED TO WEAR THEM A LOT TO BREAK THEM IN.

OH. I THOUGHT MAYBE YOU DIDN'T OWN ANOTHER PAIR OF SHOES.

GIGGLE

GIGGLE

I THOUGHT SHE **LIKED** MY BOOTS.

86

I GUESS, LIKE AT FAIRE, I'M STILL FIGURING OUT MY "CHARACTER" AND WHO I'M SUPPOSED TO BE.

EXCEPT MIDDLE SCHOOL IS A LOT WEIRDER THAN FAIRE. YOU JUST NEVER KNOW WHAT'S GOING TO HAPPEN ON ANY GIVEN DAY.

FIGHT! FIGHT!

WHERE **AM** I?! THIS PLACE IS BARBARIC!

I HANG OUT WITH MIKA MOST OF THE TIME, AND SHE HANGS OUT WITH SASHA AND EMILY. GROUPS FEEL SAFER SOMEHOW.

ME

SAFETY BUFFER

IT'S NICE TO HAVE A GROUP AROUND ME, EVEN IF SOME OF THEM ARE A LITTLE ANNOYING. I MOSTLY KIND OF SIT BACK AND WATCH SO I CAN LEARN THE RULES.

RULE # 4,062: WHEN YOU'RE ALL ALONE, THAT'S WHEN KIDS SEEM TO PICK ON YOU.

PFFFFT!

HEY, YOU KNOW THAT GIRL ANITA IN OUR SCIENCE CLASS?

ANITA WALKER? DON'T EVEN TALK TO ME ABOUT HER.

SHE THINKS SHE'S BETTER THAN EVERYONE ELSE BECAUSE SHE'S, LIKE, A GENIUS. SHE'S A TOTAL TEACHER'S PET.

ONCE, IN FOURTH GRADE, A BUNCH OF KIDS PLAYED A TRICK ON OUR TEACHER AND HID HER LITTLE STUFFED FROG THINGIE. ANITA TOLD ON US AND WE ALL GOT IN **BIG** TROUBLE.

OH.

BUT THAT WAS **FOURTH GRADE**—WHY DID THEY STILL CARE ABOUT THAT?

RULE #4,063: EVERYONE WEARS THE SAME KIND OF SHOES.

HEY EMILY, WHAT KIND OF SHOES ARE THOSE?

THEY'RE SAMMIES. THEY'RE REALLY HIGH QUALITY AND COMFORTABLE. YOU SHOULD GET SOME!

THE BEST PART OF MY DAY IS WHEN I COME HOME, ESPECIALLY ON AFTERNOONS WHEN WE GO TO THE SHOPPE TO SET UP FOR THE WEEKEND. THE FAIRE IS CLOSED TO THE PUBLIC THEN, SO I DON'T HAVE TO WORRY IF I'M DOING OR SAYING OR WEARING THE WRONG THING. IT'S LIKE I CAN BREATHE AGAIN.

AHHHHH.

OF COURSE, WEEKDAYS AT THE FAIRE AREN'T **QUITE** AS FUN AS THEY USED TO BE.

I AM STEALING YOUR CHILDREN! THE WELL WENCHES NEED SOME VICTIMS, I MEAN, VOLUNTEERS FOR A NEW ACT THEY'RE TRYING OUT!

YIPEEEE!

IMPY? DON'T YOU HAVE HOMEWORK TO DO?

AW, MAN.

HA! BETTER YOU THAN ME!

BETTER YOU THAN ME!

•GRUMBLE•

IT'S FUNNY—WHEN I DECIDED TO GO TO SCHOOL, THE ONE THING I DIDN'T REALLY THINK ABOUT WAS... THE **SCHOOL** PART.

MOST OF MY CLASSES WERE EASY AND I COULD BREEZE RIGHT THROUGH THE HOMEWORK. ENGLISH? HISTORY? NOOOO PROBLEM.

MY MATH TEACHER SEEMS LIKE SHE CHECKED OUT YEARS AGO, SO SHE DOESN'T GIVE MUCH HOMEWORK.

SPANISH—MUY FÁCIL (GRACIAS, PAPA). NO HOMEWORK IN ART OR PE, WHICH LEFT...

SCIENCE.

THUD

Read Chapter 4 (pages 55-74) and answer the following questions:

1. Which of the following is not an attribute of a planet?

a) It is not large enough to cause thermonuclear fusion.

b) It has cleared its neighboring region of planetesimals.

cont'd

HOW COULD **DOCTOR** MACGREGOR MAKE EVEN THE **PLANETS** SEEM BORING?

Boring is my super power

CLANG! CLANG!

BACK, YOU SCALLYWAG!

I'M ALL DONE, MOM! SEE YOU LATER!

DOCTOR MACGREGOR COULD WAIT.

I REGRETTED MY LIFE CHOICES THE NEXT MORNING.

DID YOU ANSWER THOSE QUESTIONS FOR SCIENCE?

OH, FIE!

WHAT?

I MEAN, OH NO! I FORGOT! I WAS KIND OF... PREOCCUPIED LAST NIGHT.

DOING WHAT?

UM...

I JUST...FORGOT.

THAT'S RIGHT, I **STILL** HAVEN'T TOLD MIKA ABOUT FAIRE YET. I KNOW WE'RE SUPPOSED TO BE FRIENDS, BUT SOMEHOW IT SEEMED SAFER TO KEEP SCHOOL AND FAIRE SEPARATE, IF YOU SEE WHAT I MEAN.

DON'T WORRY, YOU CAN BORROW MINE—THEY WERE SUPER EASY.

ARE YOU SURE?

SURE. WE'RE FRIENDS, RIGHT?

FRIENDS!!!

ONE PERSON WHO IS **NOT** HARD TO UNDERSTAND AT SCHOOL: DR. MACGREGOR. THE MAN IS PURE EVIL.

I AM VERY DISAPPOINTED WITH THE RESULTS OF THE FIRST QUIZ.

REMEMBER, IF YOU HAVE A **C OR BELOW**, YOU MUST HAVE A LEGAL GUARDIAN SIGN YOUR TEST BY MONDAY.

OH, FIE!

Imogene
Per. 4

D

I RECOMMEND YOU TAKE A LOOK AT THE EXTRA CREDIT SHEET I AM NOW HANDING OUT. THIS IS A **STAR MAP**. ON THE EVENINGS OR WEEKENDS, YOU MAY TAKE YOUR STAR MAP AND MARK ANY CONSTELLATIONS YOU SEE.

ARE THERE ALTERNATIVE ASSIGNMENTS IF WE ARE UNABLE TO DEVOTE EXCESS TIME TO STARGAZING ON WEEKNIGHTS OR WEEKENDS?

WHY IS **SHE** SO BUSY? DO YOU THINK SHE'S GOING ON HOT DATES?

GIGGLE

GIGGLE

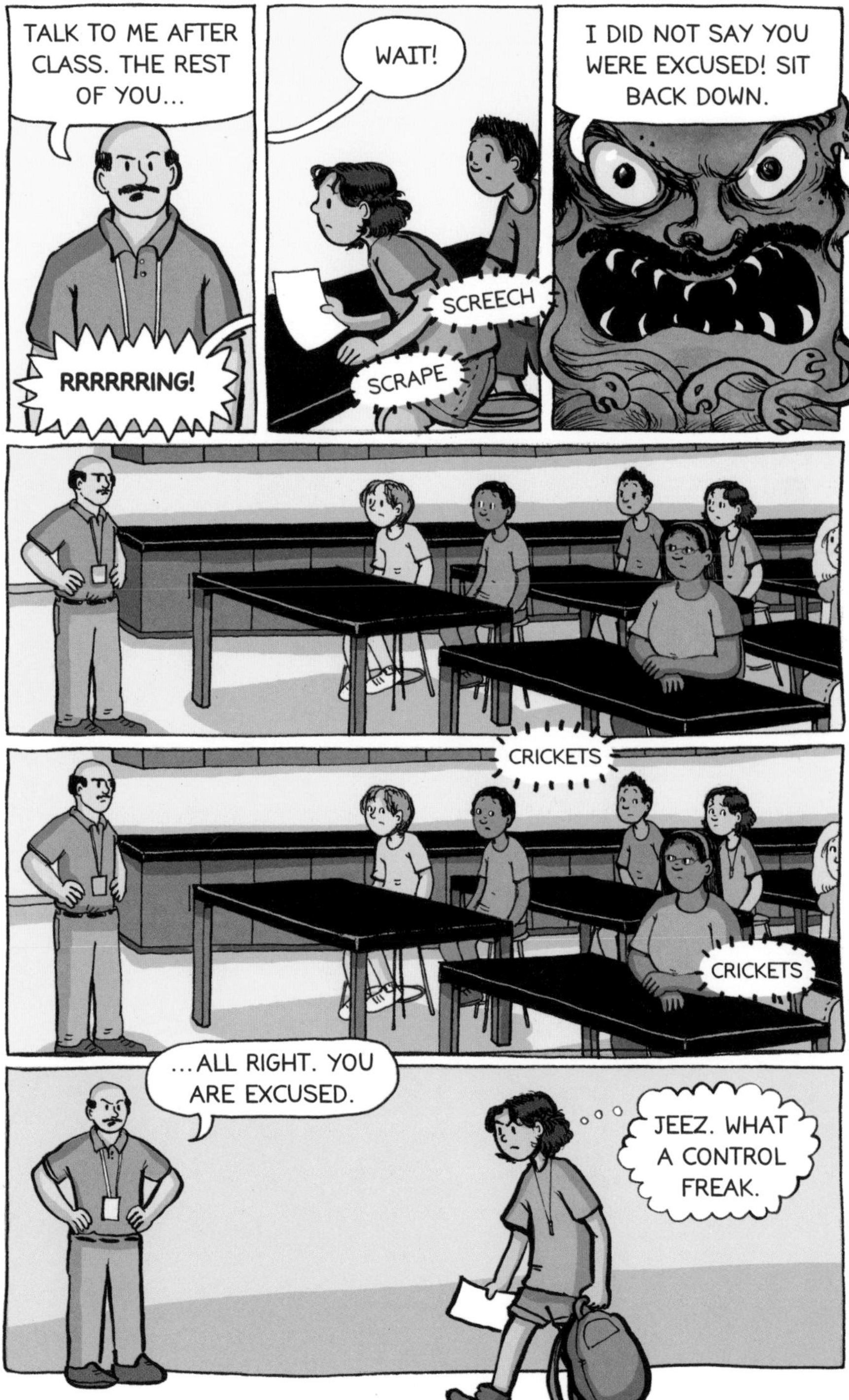
TALK TO ME AFTER CLASS. THE REST OF YOU...
RRRRRRING!
WAIT!
SCREECH
SCRAPE
I DID NOT SAY YOU WERE EXCUSED! SIT BACK DOWN.
CRICKETS
CRICKETS
...ALL RIGHT. YOU ARE EXCUSED.
JEEZ. WHAT A CONTROL FREAK.

I WASN'T **THAT** WORRIED ABOUT TELLING MY PARENTS ABOUT THE D ON MY SCIENCE TEST. THEY DIDN'T BELIEVE IN SCHOOL ANYWAY. IF WORSE CAME TO WORST, I COULD JUST GO BACK TO HOMESCHOOLING.

STILL, IT'S NOT LIKE I WAS **DYING** TO TELL THEM EITHER.

UM, MOM?

OH, RATS.

IMPY, I KNOW YOU'RE STUDYING, BUT WOULD YOU MIND RUNNING OVER TO THE WOOD SHOP AND SEEING IF GARY HAS ANY SCRAPS LYING AROUND? I WANT TO BUILD A NEW SHELF FOR THESE FAIRY HOUSES.

HEY, NO PROBLEM, MOM!

NO HARM IN GETTING ON HER GOOD SIDE BEFORE GIVING HER THE BAD NEWS.

TAKE WHATEVER YOU WANT FROM THAT PILE! IT'S ALL SCRAP.

REALLY? EVEN THIS SHIELD?

YEAH. TURNED OUT TERRIBLE.

GARY IS A BIT OF A PERFECTIONIST.

THANKS, GARY!

THE DOCTOR COULD WAIT AGAIN, BECAUSE I HAD AN IDEA FOR MY STREET CHARACTER ROUTINE.

K.I.T. SCHOOL

Chivalry

Honesty

Bravery

Juggling

"K.I.T.," EH? NAME IT AFTER SOMEONE IN PARTICULAR? A TALL, JUGGLING SOMEONE, PERHAPS?

K.I.T. SCHOOL

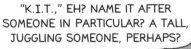

NO. FOR YOUR INFORMATION, IT STANDS FOR "KNIGHT-IN-TRAINING" SCHOOL. I CAN TEACH KIDS HOW TO SWORD FIGHT AND JUGGLE. I'LL SET UP ON THAT CORNER OVER THERE—AND MOM, WHENEVER YOU SELL A WOODEN SWORD YOU CAN SEND THE KIDS OVER TO ME! YOU MIGHT WANT TO START SELLING JUGGLING KITS TOO.

QUITE THE HEAD FOR BUSINESS, THIS ONE! FUTURE CEO, EH, IMPY? DON'T FORGET US LITTLE PEOPLE WHEN YOU MAKE YOUR FIRST MILLION.

HMMMM! CEO **DOES** HAVE A NICE RING TO IT.

IT'S A GOOD IDEA, IMPY. I'M PROUD OF HOW YOU'RE HANDLING EVERYTHING—SCHOOL, YOUR SQUIRE DUTIES. MY BRAVE LITTLE TOASTER. COME SIT BY ME, I'LL FRENCH BRAID YOUR HAIR.

MOM!!

IT'S EMBARRASSING WHEN SHE USES HER OLD NICKNAME FOR ME!

(...EVEN IF I DON'T **REALLY** MIND.)

I DECIDED NOT TO WORRY ABOUT MY SCIENCE TEST RIGHT NOW. IT **WAS** THE WEEKEND, AFTER ALL.

UNLIKE SCHOOL DAYS, I WAKE UP READY AND EXCITED FOR THE DAY ON FAIRE WEEKENDS.

RIGHT AWAY, K.I.T. WAS A BIG HIT! KIDS SEEMED TO LIKE IT. PARENTS SEEMED TO LIKE IT. EVEN THE QUEEN STOPPED BY!

I SEE THE RUMORS ARE TRUE—THOU ART TRAINING THE NEXT GENERATION OF FAITHFUL SERVANTS TO THE KINGDOM!

TELL ME, BRAVE KNIGHTS-IN-TRAINING, ARE YOU READY TO HELP DEFEND THE KINGDOM AGAINST THIS TERRIBLE DRAGON THAT THREATENS US?

YES!!

I HAVE A SWORD!

I HAVE A DRAGON PAINTED ON MY FACE, LOOK!

I SAW A DRAGON ONCE!

97

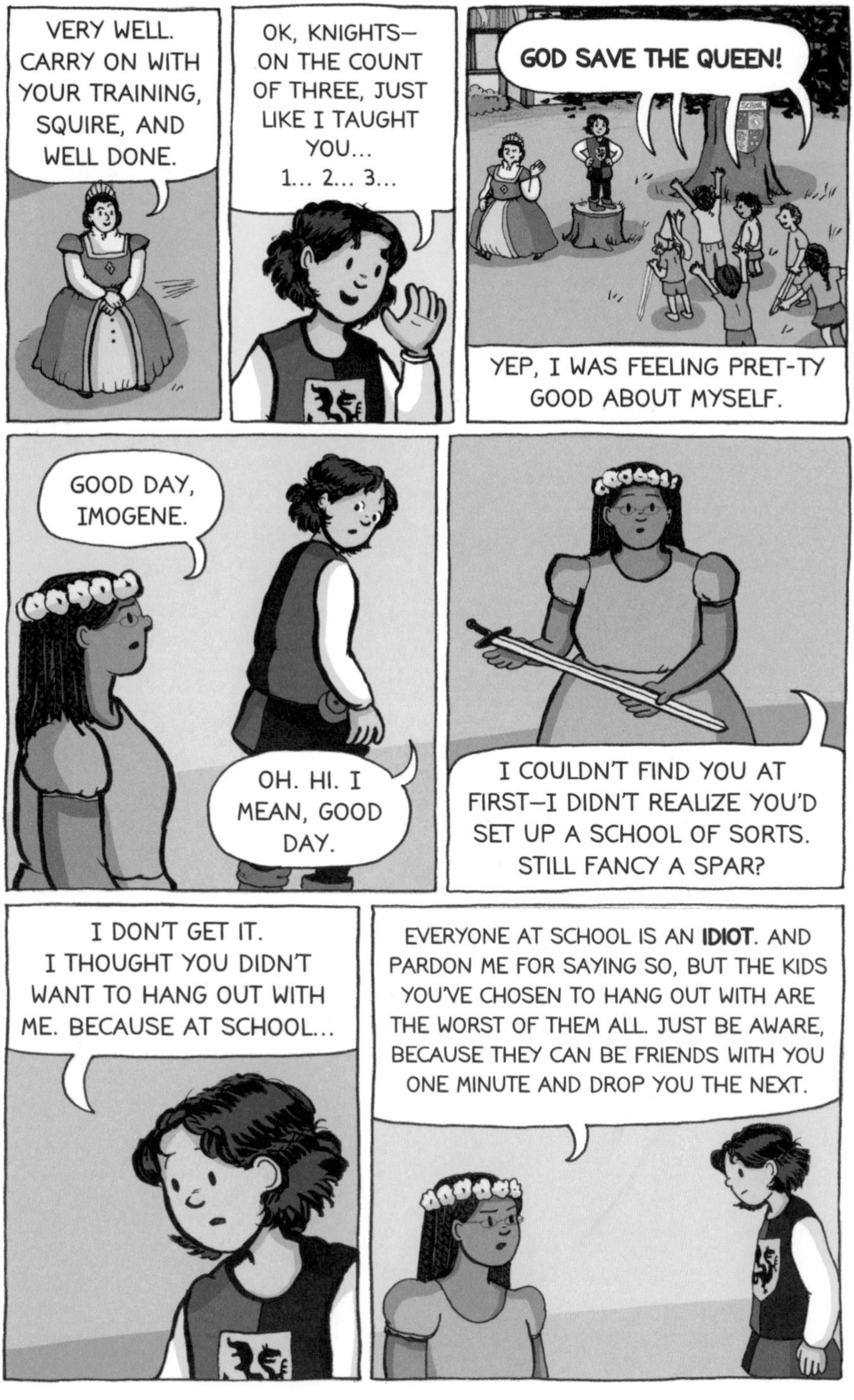
VERY WELL. CARRY ON WITH YOUR TRAINING, SQUIRE, AND WELL DONE.
OK, KNIGHTS— ON THE COUNT OF THREE, JUST LIKE I TAUGHT YOU... 1... 2... 3...
GOD SAVE THE QUEEN!
SCHOOL
YEP, I WAS FEELING PRET-TY GOOD ABOUT MYSELF.
GOOD DAY, IMOGENE.
OH. HI. I MEAN, GOOD DAY.
I COULDN'T FIND YOU AT FIRST—I DIDN'T REALIZE YOU'D SET UP A SCHOOL OF SORTS. STILL FANCY A SPAR?
I DON'T GET IT. I THOUGHT YOU DIDN'T WANT TO HANG OUT WITH ME. BECAUSE AT SCHOOL...
EVERYONE AT SCHOOL IS AN **IDIOT**. AND PARDON ME FOR SAYING SO, BUT THE KIDS YOU'VE CHOSEN TO HANG OUT WITH ARE THE WORST OF THEM ALL. JUST BE AWARE, BECAUSE THEY CAN BE FRIENDS WITH YOU ONE MINUTE AND DROP YOU THE NEXT.

THEY DON'T SEEM **THAT** BAD. OK, THEY CAN BE A LITTLE SHALLOW SOMETIMES, BUT OVERALL THEY'RE PRETTY NICE...

I'VE KNOWN THEM FOR MOST OF MY LIFE, AND TRUST ME— THEY'RE IDIOTS. WHY DO YOU THINK I WORK SO HARD AT SCHOOL? I'M GOING TO BE VALEDICTORIAN, AND THEN I'M GOING TO GO TO AN IVY LEAGUE SCHOOL AND MOVE FAR, FAR AWAY. ONLY SEVEN MORE YEARS.

SO, I REPEAT: DO YOU FANCY A SPAR?

IT'S REALLY HARD TO TURN DOWN A GOOD SWORD FIGHT WITH A FORMIDABLE OPPONENT.

Training Swords

A LITTLE SWORDPLAY TAKES YOUR MIND OFF ANY PROBLEM. AND ANITA WAS GOOD—**REALLY** GOOD! I'M GOOD IN A SHOWY SORT OF WAY, BUT SHE ACTUALLY KNEW WHAT SHE WAS DOING.

A FINE AND NOBLE FIGHT!

YOU KNOW, YOU **ARE** QUITE LUCKY TO WORK HERE. WHEN I WAS A CHILD I DREAMED OF BEING IN ONE OF THE SWORD-FIGHTING SHOWS.

I BET YOU COULD! YOU'RE REALLY GOOD!

I WANT TO LEARN HOW TO DO THAT!

TEACH ME! TEACH ME!

QUIET! HOLD ON A SEC, THERE ARE TOO MANY OF YOU!

YOU THREE, COME OVER HERE. IMOGENE, HAVE YOU GOT THE REST?

RULE #4,065: IT'S OK TO BE FRIENDS WITH SOMEONE **OUTSIDE** OF SCHOOL, EVEN IF YOU'RE NOT FRIENDS **IN** SCHOOL...I GUESS?

THIS SEEMED LIKE A WEIRD RULE.

CHAPTER SIX

If you yourself find thyself embarked upon a journey into unexplored territory, you may meet fellow travelers or local townsfolk along the way. It may be interesting to get to know the ways of these people—visit their homes and learn their local customs, so that you might feel more at ease in a strange new land.

SINCE ANITA DIDN'T WANT TO TALK IN SCHOOL, I JUST WATCHED HER IN CLASS ON MONDAY.

ALWAYS RAISING HAND

WEIRD GUMMY ERASER ANIMALS

TUCKED-IN T-SHIRT

WHY DOESN'T SHE JUST *TRY* TO BLEND IN A LITTLE MORE?

I GUESS I COULD SEE WHY OTHER KIDS MADE FUN OF HER. SHE *DID* KIND OF STAND OUT.

IF YOU HAVE A TEST YOU HAD TO HAVE SIGNED, PLEASE LEAVE IT IN THE BOX AFTER CLASS.

OH FIE! I COMPLETELY FORGOT!

IT'S NOT LIKE HE **KNOWS** WHAT MY PARENTS' SIGNATURES LOOK LIKE.

MS. VEGA! I ASKED YOU A QUESTION!

AGHHHH!

PLEASE SEE ME AFTER CLASS.

WE JUST READ SILENTLY AFTER THAT.

WHEN THE BELL RANG, *THE DOCTOR* KEPT GRADING HIS PAPERS AND PRETENDED LIKE HE DIDN'T SEE ME.

AHEM

EXCUSE ME, DR. MACGREGOR?

MS. VEGA. YOU ARE COMING TO US FROM A HOMESCHOOLING SITUATION, IS THAT CORRECT?

I'M CONCERNED ABOUT YOUR PERFORMANCE IN THIS CLASS. YOUR ASSIGNMENTS ARE INCOMPLETE, YOUR CLASS PARTICIPATION... NONEXISTENT. I'M NOT SURE WHAT TYPE OF INSTRUCTION YOU HAD BEFORE...

BUT IN MIDDLE SCHOOL I EXPECT MORE FROM MY PUPILS.

AND **I** EXPECTED A TEACHER WHO ACTUALLY TEACHES US STUFF, INSTEAD OF MAKING US READ BY OURSELVES ALL THE TIME!

ARE WE CLEAR?

HMM? YES, SIR.

I ALMOST BOWED, BUT I STOPPED MYSELF JUST IN TIME. **THAT** WOULD HAVE BEEN EMBARRASSING!

WHAT A JERK. NO WONDER MY PARENTS DIDN'T WANT TO SEND ME TO PUBLIC SCHOOL.

IMOGENE! WHAT DID HE SAY TO YOU?

NOTHING. UGGH, I HATE HIM SO MUCH!

YEAH, HE'S THE WORST. HEY, I ALMOST FORGOT. DO YOU WANT TO COME TO MY HOUSE AFTER SCHOOL? MY MOM FINALLY GOT MY INVITATIONS—WE'RE GOING TO PLAN MY BIRTHDAY PARTY!

TODAY?

THE TRUTH WAS...THE IDEA OF GOING TO MIKA'S HOUSE TERRIFIED ME. IT WAS HARD ENOUGH KNOWING HOW TO ACT EIGHT HOURS A DAY AT SCHOOL. WHAT I *REALLY* WANTED TO DO WAS GO HOME, EAT A NICE BOWL OF CEREAL, AND RELAX.

BUT I WAS *SUPPOSED* TO WANT TO HANG OUT WITH KIDS FROM SCHOOL...RIGHT?

I GUESS SO?

GEEZ, DON'T SOUND **TOO** EXCITED! WE'RE MEETING AT MY LOCKER AFTER SCHOOL.

I RODE MIKA'S BUS HOME THAT AFTERNOON INSTEAD OF MINE.

IT TURNS OUT, EMILY AND A BUNCH OF OTHER KIDS RODE HER BUS, TOO.

MAYBE IT WAS THANKS TO ANITA...BUT I COULDN'T QUITE FIGURE OUT WHY MIKA WANTED TO HANG OUT WITH ME. WE DIDN'T HAVE THAT MUCH IN COMMON.

CLOTHES

MAKEUP

BOYS

YOU'RE SO QUIET, IMOGENE! WHY ARE YOU SO QUIET?

THAT'S A TERRIBLE QUESTION TO ASK SOMEONE. NOW I FELT EVEN **MORE** NERVOUS AND QUIET.

C'MON IMOGENE, THIS IS OUR STOP.

YOU LIVE **HERE**?

WE SOMETIMES DROVE AROUND THIS DEVELOPMENT TO LOOK AT MANSIONS. I NEVER EXPECTED TO GO *IN* ONE.

LET'S GET A SNACK BEFORE WE GO TO MY ROOM.

HER KITCHEN LOOKED LIKE A GROCERY STORE. WE **NEVER** HAD SUCH GOOD SNACKS AT MY HOUSE—ALL OF THIS WOULD BE GONE IN ABOUT FIVE MINUTES AFTER IT CAME THROUGH THE DOOR.

YOU HAVE SO MANY **SHOES**!

I HAVE EVERY COLOR OF SAMMIES THAT THEY MAKE.

OK, FIRST THINGS FIRST, WE HAVE TO MAKE A GUEST LIST. SASHA, YOU WRITE IT DOWN.

YOU DON'T HAVE TO JUST **STAND** THERE, IMOGENE. YOU CAN SIT DOWN.

GIGGLE

OK, GUEST LIST. SO THERE'S ME. THE THREE OF YOU.

WHAT ABOUT LAUREN?

NO. SHE'S DEAD TO ME.

WASN'T THAT THE GIRL YOU WERE JUST TALKING TO ON THE BUS?

MIKA SHOT ME A LOOK. SOMETHING **ELSE** I DIDN'T UNDERSTAND, APPARENTLY.

THEN KAIDEN, OBVIOUSLY.

AND RYAN.

AND TYLER!

GIGGLE

GIGGLE

AND JASON!

OOOOO!

ADMIT IT, IMOGENE. YOU LIKE HIM, DON'T YOU.

EWW! NO I **DON'T**.

HE LIKES **YOU**. IT'S SO OBVIOUS. YOU **HAVE** TO GIVE HIM THE INVITATION TOMORROW.

NO WAY.

YES WAY. YOU'RE UNINVITED IF YOU DON'T DO IT. IT'S DECIDED.

BUT...

AND SPEAKING OF ROMANCE...LOOK WHAT **I** HAVE...

OH, YOU READ ANIMAL ANTICS? I READ THOSE TOO, I LOVE THEM!

YOU DO? ME TOO!

DID YOU READ THE ONE...

YOU GUYS, FORGET ABOUT THAT. THOSE ARE REALLY OLD. LOOK AT **THIS**! I FOUND IT IN MY SISTER'S ROOM.

IT'S ABOUT THIS GIRL WHO MOVED TO CALIFORNIA TO BECOME AN ACTRESS. THIS IS THE BEST PART!

"SYDNEY SHIVERED AS TYLER TOOK HER HAND AND LED HER INTO THE WARM, GENTLE OCEAN.

"HIS HANDS MOVED TO HER BACK AND SLOWLY UNTIED THE NECK OF HER WHITE HALTER BIKINI TOP."

THIS WAS ALL WAY, WAY TOO MUCH. I DIDN'T BELONG HERE—I WANTED TO GO HOME.

BUT I SORT OF WANTED TO HEAR MORE...WHAT WAS **WRONG** WITH ME?

KNOCK-KNOCK!

EEEEEEEE!

IMOGENE, TAKE THIS FOR ME!

SHOVE

HERE ARE YOUR INVITATIONS, MIKA. ...WHAT ARE YOU ALL UP TO?

NOTHING!

I'M LEAVING. CALL YOUR DAD IF YOU NEED ANYTHING, AND IF HE DOESN'T ANSWER...TELL HIM IT'S **HIS** WEEK WITH YOU AND YOUR SISTER. AND I WANT YOUR FRIENDS HOME BY FIVE O'CLOCK.

OKAY, MOM!

WOW. OTHER FAMILIES ARE WEIRD.

ARE YOU GUYS READY TO SEE MY INVITATIONS?

"YE ARE CORDIALLY INVITED..."

WAAIITT...WHERE IS YOUR BIRTHDAY PARTY GOING TO BE?

IT'S GOING TO BE...

AT THE RENAISSANCE FAIRE!

WAIT. YOU...**LIKE** THE RENAISSANCE FAIRE?

OK, MAYBE IT **SOUNDS** DORKY, BUT IT'S ACTUALLY **REALLY** FUN. MY DAD TOOK ME A FEW YEARS AGO. YOU CAN GET YOUR HAIR BRAIDED, AND I GOT A METAL ROSE. HAVE YOU EVER BEEN?

UM, WELL. ACTUALLY... •AHEM•...THAT IS...

I GUESS IT WAS NOW OR NEVER. MAYBE THEY WOULD THINK IT WAS COOL. AND I COULDN'T KEEP IT A SECRET FOREVER.

ACTUALLY...MY FAMILY WORKS THERE. LIKE, MY MOM AND DAD. AND I HELP. AROUND THE SHOPPE. WITH MY LITTLE BROTHER.

THAT'S PROBABLY THE MOST WORDS I'VE SAID TO MIKA AT ONE TIME.

NO WAY!

UMM, THAT'S.... COOL, I GUESS.

I THOUGHT IT WAS, LIKE, CARNIES WHO WORKED THERE.

WELL, SOME PEOPLE TRAVEL AROUND. BUT MY MOM OWNS A SHOPPE, AND MY DAD IS A KNIGHT. HE'S AN ACTOR.

YOUR DAD'S A **KNIGHT**?

YOUR DAD'S AN **ACTOR**? HAS HE BEEN ON TV?

•WHEW• THEY **SEEMED** TO BE TAKING THIS PRETTY WELL...I THINK?

HE WAS IN SOME COMMERCIALS A FEW YEARS AGO, BUT NOW HE JUST WORKS LOCALLY.

THEY STARTED TALKING ABOUT ACTORS AND TV SHOWS THEN, AND I RELAXED A LITTLE BIT. I FELT BETTER NOW THAT MY SECRET WAS OUT.

BUT IT SEEMED LIKE MIKA WAS LOOKING AT ME— AND MY BOOTS—A LITTLE DIFFERENTLY NOW.

IT TURNS OUT SASHA LIVES KIND OF NEAR ME, SO AT 4:45 HER MOM DROVE ME HOME.

OUR APARTMENT COMPLEX SUDDENLY LOOKED A LOT SHABBIER.

I'LL WAIT HERE UNTIL YOU GET INSIDE.

THAT'S OK. YOU DON'T HAVE TO.

IT'S NO PROBLEM. IT WAS NICE MEETING YOU, IMOGENE.

SEE YOU TOMORROW!

HEY, THAT'S WEIRD...

JIGGLE

JIGGLE

KNOCK

KNOCK

MOM! I CAN'T OPEN THE DOOR!

MAGIC WORD, WHAT IS?

OH, NO.

EVEN THOUGH HE'S SEEN *STAR WARS* ABOUT 2.5 MILLION TIMES, FELIX'S YODA IMPERSONATION IS TRULY TERRIBLE.

LET ME IN!

MAGIC WORD, IT IS NOT!

SLAM!

MOM? MOM! FELIX WON'T LET ME IN!

BANG!

BANG!

AT THE POST OFFICE, IS SHE!

RATS! THE CAR IS MISSING!

DAD! LET ME IN!

IN THE BATHROOM, IS HE! IN THERE FOR AN HOUR, WILL HE BE!

OPEN UP! OPEN THIS DOOR, YOU GOBLIN!

BANG! BANG! BANG! BANG! BANG!

YOU MUST LEARN PATIENCE, MY CHILD, PATIE—**AGGGGH!**

FELIX, OPEN THE DOOR! WHAT IS WRONG WITH YOU?

FELIX! GO TO YOUR ROOM!

AAAAAAAAGH!

RRRRRRGGHGHHH! THAT'S **SO** HUMILIATING! A GIRL FROM SCHOOL WAS WATCHING THAT! WHY DOES HE HAVE TO BE SO ANNOYING?

THAT'S THE JOB OF A LITTLE BROTHER.

I DIDN'T EVEN **SEE** MIKA'S SISTER—**THAT'S** THE KIND OF SIBLING I WANT.

IT'S "FEND FOR YOURSELF" NIGHT FOR DINNER. IF YOU CAN FIND IT, YOU CAN EAT IT.

I **HATE** "FEND FOR YOURSELF" NIGHT. I ALWAYS END UP WITH A HANDFUL OF CROUTONS AND MAYBE—JUST MAYBE—A SLICE OF PRE-WRAPPED CHEESE.

115

IT'S KIND OF MESSY IN HERE, DON'T YOU THINK?

OH, ARE YOU OFFERING TO CLEAN UP? HOW WONDERFUL, THANK YOU.

I'LL JUST...BE IN MY ROOM.

UH-HUH.

I **TRIED** TO START MY HOMEWORK...

STUPID EXTRA CREDIT—I CAN'T SEE **ANY** STARS. ALL I SEE ARE THE LIGHTS FROM THE PARKING LOT.

"TYLER SLID SYDNEY'S HALTER TOP OFF HER TANNED SHOULDERS..."

KNOCK KNOCK

IMPY! CLOTHES DELIVERY.

AAAAGH!

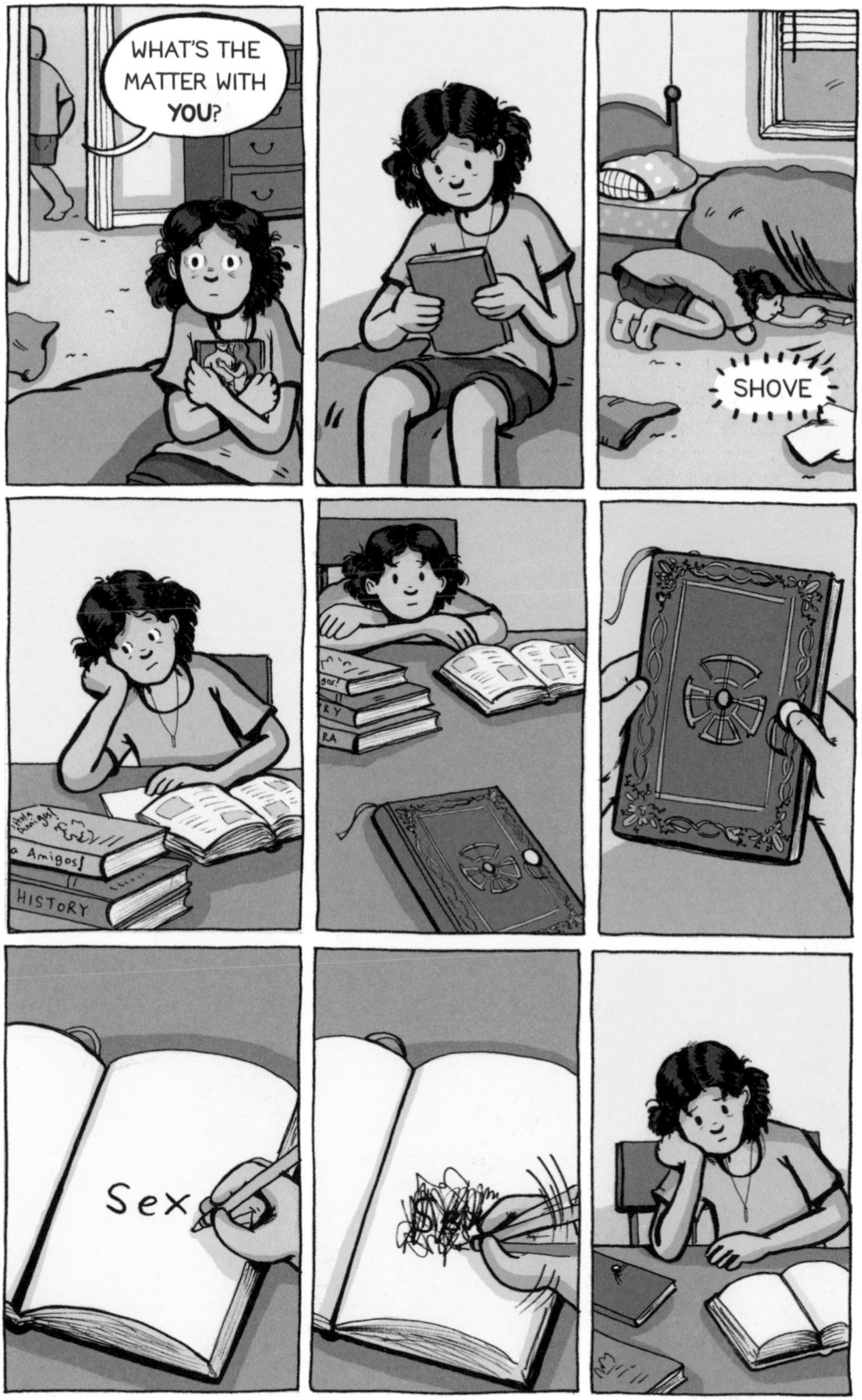
WHAT'S THE MATTER WITH YOU?
SHOVE
¡Hola Amigos!
HISTORY
Sex

AS I GOT READY FOR SCHOOL THE NEXT MORNING...

HMMM...

IF YOU'RE A KID, YOU MIGHT BE FAMILIAR WITH THIS DILEMMA. YOU NEED TO ASK A FAVOR AND YOU HAVE TO DECIDE WHICH PARENT IS MORE LIKELY TO SAY YES.

I DID A QUICK MENTAL CALCULATION.

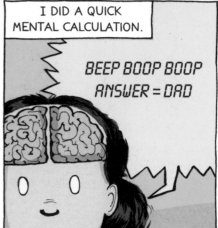

BEEP BOOP BOOP
ANSWER = DAD

HEY DAD, WHEN DO I GET MY NEXT PAYCHECK FOR BEING A SQUIRE? I NEED TO GET A NEW PAIR OF SHOES.

NEW SHOES? WHAT'S WRONG WITH YOUR BOOTS?

OH FIE. THIS WAS NOT PART OF THE PLAN.

RECALCULATING.
RECALCULATING.

NOTHING'S WRONG WITH MY BOOTS. I JUST NEED A PAIR OF SNEAKERS.

...FOR PE. WE ALL NEED SNEAKERS FOR PE.

I DON'T USUALLY LIE TO MY PARENTS...BUT THE WHOLE SAMMIE THING SEEMED TOO COMPLICATED TO EXPLAIN.

•TSK• IMPY, IF YOU NEED SNEAKERS FOR PE YOU DON'T NEED TO BUY THEM YOURSELF! WE'LL PICK SOME UP ON OUR WAY TO FAIRE TONIGHT.

THAT WAS EASY!

THANKS, MOM! YOU'RE THE MOST WONDERFUL MOTHER IN THE WHOLE WIDE WORLD!

MM-HMM.

I WAS PRETTY NERVOUS ABOUT SCHOOL TODAY. I WONDERED IF OTHER KIDS WOULD FIND OUT ABOUT THE FAIRE THING.

SHORT ANSWER: YES.

THIS IS CALLED A "WATCH." IT'S A MODERN INVENTION THAT TELLS TIME.

HA-HA.

I DIDN'T FEEL LIKE TELLING HER THEY ACTUALLY **HAD** WATCHES DURING THE RENAISSANCE.

SO DO YOU SWORD-FIGHT AND STUFF?

UM, SOMETIMES. I CAN JUGGLE TOO.

THAT'S COOL!

SEE? HE **LIKES** YOU. AFTER SCHOOL YOU'RE GIVING HIM THE INVITATION.

GULP

THERE'S ABOUT TEN MINUTES AFTER SCHOOL BEFORE THE BUSES LEAVE. USUALLY I GET RIGHT ON MY BUS, BUT SINCE MOM WAS PICKING ME UP TODAY...

JASON'S STANDING RIGHT OVER THERE. GO GIVE IT TO HIM!

UH, I THINK I SEE MY MOM—I HAVE TO GO.

GO. DO IT FAST, LIKE RIPPING OFF A BAND-AID.

HONK HONK!

OH, NO.

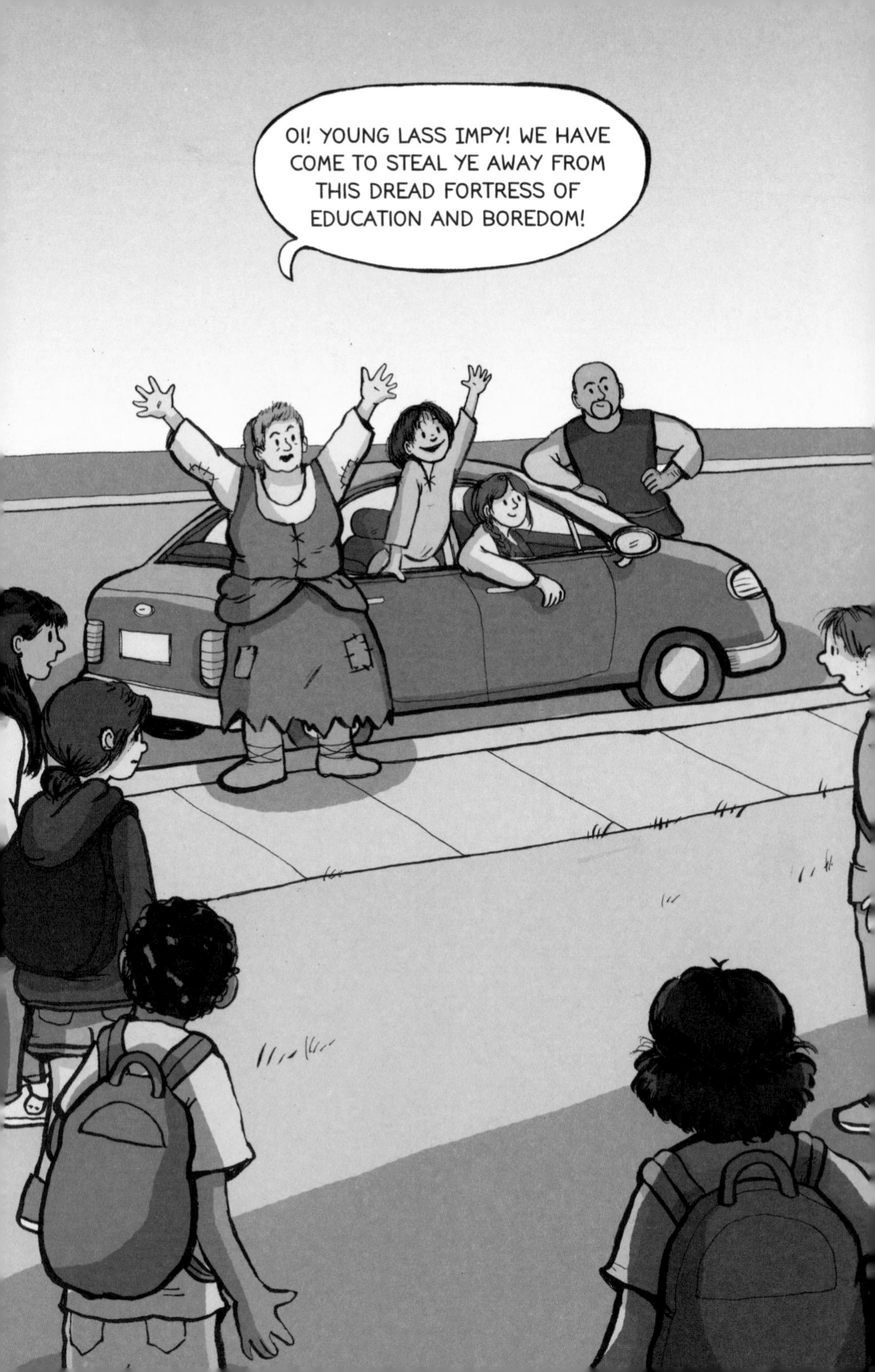
OI! YOUNG LASS IMPY! WE HAVE COME TO STEAL YE AWAY FROM THIS DREAD FORTRESS OF EDUCATION AND BOREDOM!

HERE.

DASH

WHAT ARE YOU ALL **DOING** HERE?

I NEVER PASS UP A TRIP TO VALU-MART! I NEED SOME NEW **BRASSIERES**!

OH MY GOSH. COULD YOU KEEP IT DOWN, PLEASE? YOU'RE EMBARRASSING ME!

EMBARRASSING YOU? GOOD HEAVENS, WE WOULDN'T WANT TO **EMBARRASS** YOU!

AWAY, O TRUSTY WAGON! AWAY FROM THIS INSTITUTION OF BRAINWASHING OF OUR YOUTH! O SCHOOL, WE BLOW FARTS IN YOUR GENERAL DIRECTION!

OH MY GOSH.

LIGHTEN UP, IMPY! LIVE A LITTLE!

EASY FOR **YOU** TO SAY! I HAVE TO GO BACK THERE!

IS EVERYONE GOING IN? DRESSED LIKE **THIS**?

WE'VE DONE THIS A HUNDRED TIMES, IMPY! WHAT'S THE MATTER WITH YOU TODAY?

GEE, I DON'T KNOW—JUST THAT ONE OF THE KIDS FROM MY **SCHOOL** MIGHT BE HERE?

YOU KNOW, SCHOOL IS TURNING YOU INTO A REAL STICK-IN-THE-MUD.

I SPLIT AWAY FROM MY FAMILY AS QUICKLY AS POSSIBLE ONCE WE WERE INSIDE.

I'LL BE IN THE SHOE SECTION!

I WAS STARTING TO GET WORRIED I WOULDN'T FIND WHAT I WAS LOOKING FOR, BUT THEN...

YES!

THEY WERE A SIZE TOO SMALL, BUT THEY DIDN'T HURT TOO BADLY. MY TOES WERE JUST A LITTLE CRAMMED.

$12.99! QUITE THE BARGAIN!

OH IMPY, THESE ARE SUCH POOR QUALITY. LOOK, THE RUBBER IS ALREADY COMING AWAY FROM THE CANVAS.

MOM! THEY'RE FINE! THEY'RE THE KIND WE'RE SUPPOSED TO GET FOR CLASS!

•SIGH• I DON'T THINK...

FELIX!

DON'T YOU MOVE A MUSCLE!

THANKS, MOM—YOU'RE THE GREATEST! I'LL BE WAITING OUTSIDE!

JUST LOOKING AT MY NEW SAMMIES IN THE CAR FILLED ME WITH GREAT JOY. I KNOW, IT'S JUST A PAIR OF SHOES...BUT IN A WEIRD WAY I FELT LIKE THEY WOULD SOLVE ALL OF MY PROBLEMS.

GLEAMING HAIR

COOL, CONFIDENT ATTITUDE

WHAT A COOL AND CONFIDENT GIRL!

NITA ALWAYS CAME TO MY KNIGHT-IN-TRAINING SCHOOL NOW ON FAIRE DAYS. IT WAS FUN HAVING SOMEONE TO DO STREET WITH.

WATCH ME!

WHEN IT WAS QUIET, WE SPARRED.

LET ME TRY!

DURING MY BREAKS, WE PLAYED NINE MEN'S MORRIS.

I WANT TO PLAY!

SURE, SHE WAS STILL A **LITTLE** AGGRAVATING SOMETIMES...

SO WE EACH HAVE FIVE DOLLARS. HOW ABOUT I BUY SOUP IN A BREAD BOWL, AND YOU BUY AN APPLE DUMPLING, AND WE SHARE?

I DON'T EAT DESSERTS IN THE MIDDLE OF THE DAY. I'M GOING TO GET A TURKEY SANDWICH AND SOME FRUIT.

SIGH

WE WEREN'T BEST FRIENDS OR ANYTHING, BUT SHE ALWAYS CAME TO CHEER ALONG AT THE CHESS MATCH AND THE JOUST.

ALL IN ALL, I DIDN'T REALLY GET WHY SHE DIDN'T HAVE ANY FRIENDS AT SCHOOL.

HAVE YOU EVER THOUGHT ABOUT, YOU KNOW, **DRESSING** MORE LIKE THE OTHER KIDS AT SCHOOL?

TURNS OUT, MOM IS NOT THE ONLY ONE WHO CAN GIVE **THE LOOK**.

I **DID** WORRY A LITTLE BIT ABOUT WHAT WOULD HAPPEN WHEN MIKA CAME TO THE FAIRE FOR HER PARTY. WOULD I KEEP WORKING? OR WOULD I HANG OUT WITH THEM? WOULD THEY THINK MY COSTUME WAS STUPID?

OK, OK. IT WAS JUST A QUESTION.

I DECIDED NOT TO THINK ABOUT IT AT THE MOMENT.

HEY! KIDS! YOU WANT TO GO ON A DRAGON HUNT? REMEMBER OUR RULES OF KNIGHTHOOD: CHIVALRY HONESTY. BRAVERY. AND... LET'S GO!

THAT'S MY DAUGHTER!

NO, I WOULDN'T WORRY ABOUT MIKA'S PARTY. EVERYTHING WAS GOING SO WELL. WHAT COULD POSSIBLY GO WRONG?

CHAPTER SEVEN

Even on the most dangerous of quests, there can be moments of peace and tranquility. The sun shines fondly on your shoulders and your pack is lighter to bear. . . . Enjoy it, because it sure as heck won't last forever.

FOR ONCE, I WAS SORT OF LOOKING FORWARD TO SCHOOL! EXCEPT, MY NEW SHOES WERE SO BRIGHT—THEY WERE LIKE A BEACON OF LIGHT. **TOO** OBVIOUS, IF YOU SEE WHAT I MEAN.

SCUFF

SCUFF

IT WAS LIKE MY NEW SHOES CAST A CONFIDENCE SPELL OVER ME—I FELT LIKE I HAD A POPULARITY FORCE FIELD AROUND ME.

HI!

HEY, IMOGENE!

THIS SCHOOL THING ISN'T SO HARD. IT'S A BIT SILLY THAT ANITA NEVER TALKS TO ANYBODY HERE.

HI, ANITA!

OOH, ANITA, DID YOU FINALLY MAKE A FRIEND? IT'S JUST BECAUSE IMOGENE IS NEW HERE—SHE DOESN'T KNOW ANY BETTER.

I **TOLD** YOU, IMOGENE, LEAVE IT ALONE.

SERIOUSLY, DON'T BOTHER WITH HER.

THE SHOES AND I STOOD A LITTLE STRAIGHTER.

ACTUALLY, I THINK SHE'S PRETTY NICE.

NO, SHE ISN'T. I KNOW YOU'RE NEW TO THE WHOLE CONCEPT OF "SCHOOL" AND EVERYTHING, BUT TRUST ME ON THIS ONE.

POP

GOOD MOOD...GONE.

AND THEN IT GOT WORSE.

NEW SHOES?

UM, YEAH. I GOT SOME SAMMIES OVER THE WEEKEND.

I HATE TO BREAK IT TO YOU, BUT **THOSE** ARE NOT SAMMIES. **THESE** ARE SAMMIES.

YEAH. SO ARE THESE.

SEE THIS PURPLE STAR ON THE BACK? THAT MEANS THEY'RE **REAL** SAMMIES. YOURS ARE CHEAP KNOCK-OFFS.

SUDDENLY IT WAS 1,000 DEGREES OUTSIDE. HOW HAD I NOT NOTICED THAT?!

THEY LOOK ALMOST THE SAME TO ME! I KIND OF LIKE YOURS BETTER!

•SNORT•

REAL SAMMIES VS. FAKE SAMMIES: EXAMPLE #4,064 OF THINGS I DIDN'T UNDERSTAND ABOUT MIDDLE SCHOOL.

PUZZLER #4,065: WHY EVERYONE LIKED MIKA SO MUCH, WHEN SOMETIMES SHE COULD BE REALLY MEAN.

IMOGENE, THERE'S YOUR BEST FRIEND ANITA. DON'T YOU WANT TO SIT NEXT TO HER?

PUZZLER #4,066: WHY **I** WANTED MIKA TO LIKE ME SO MUCH, WHEN SOMETIMES SHE COULD BE REALLY MEAN.

THERE. PERFECT!

OR AS I REALIZED THE NEXT DAY...NOT SO PERFECT.

OH MY GOD, DID YOU **DRAW** PURPLE STARS ON YOUR SHOES? THAT IS ABOUT THE SADDEST THING I HAVE EVER SEEN.

PUZZLER #4,067: HOW THINGS COULD GO DOWNHILL SO QUICKLY. I **THOUGHT** I WAS STARTING TO MAKE FRIENDS. NOW I WAS PRETTY SURE I'D SCREWED EVERYTHING UP.

WHAT **HAPPENED?**

STUPID SHOES.

I MAY BE NEW TO SCHOOL, BUT EVEN **I** COULD SENSE THINGS WEREN'T GOING SO HOT FOR ME, FRIEND-WISE, AT THE MOMENT.

BELIEVE IT OR NOT, MY DAY GOT WORSE. HOW? IF YOU GUESSED "SCIENCE CLASS," GIVE YOURSELF 100 POINTS.

TODAY WE'RE GOING TO LEARN THE SYMBOLS FOR THE PLANETS, AS FIRST DESCRIBED IN MEDIEVAL BYZANTINE CODICES.

Work with your lab partner to label each symbol.

UH-OH. HE DIDN'T SMILE BACK. IS HE EMBARRASSED THAT I GAVE HIM THAT INVITATION? DID HE HEAR THE THING ABOUT MY SHOES? DOES HE NOT LIKE ME ANYMORE? DID HE **EVER** LIKE ME?

UM, I THINK THE FIRST ONE IS THE MOON.

OH. HEH-HEH. THE NEXT ONE IS NEPTUNE.

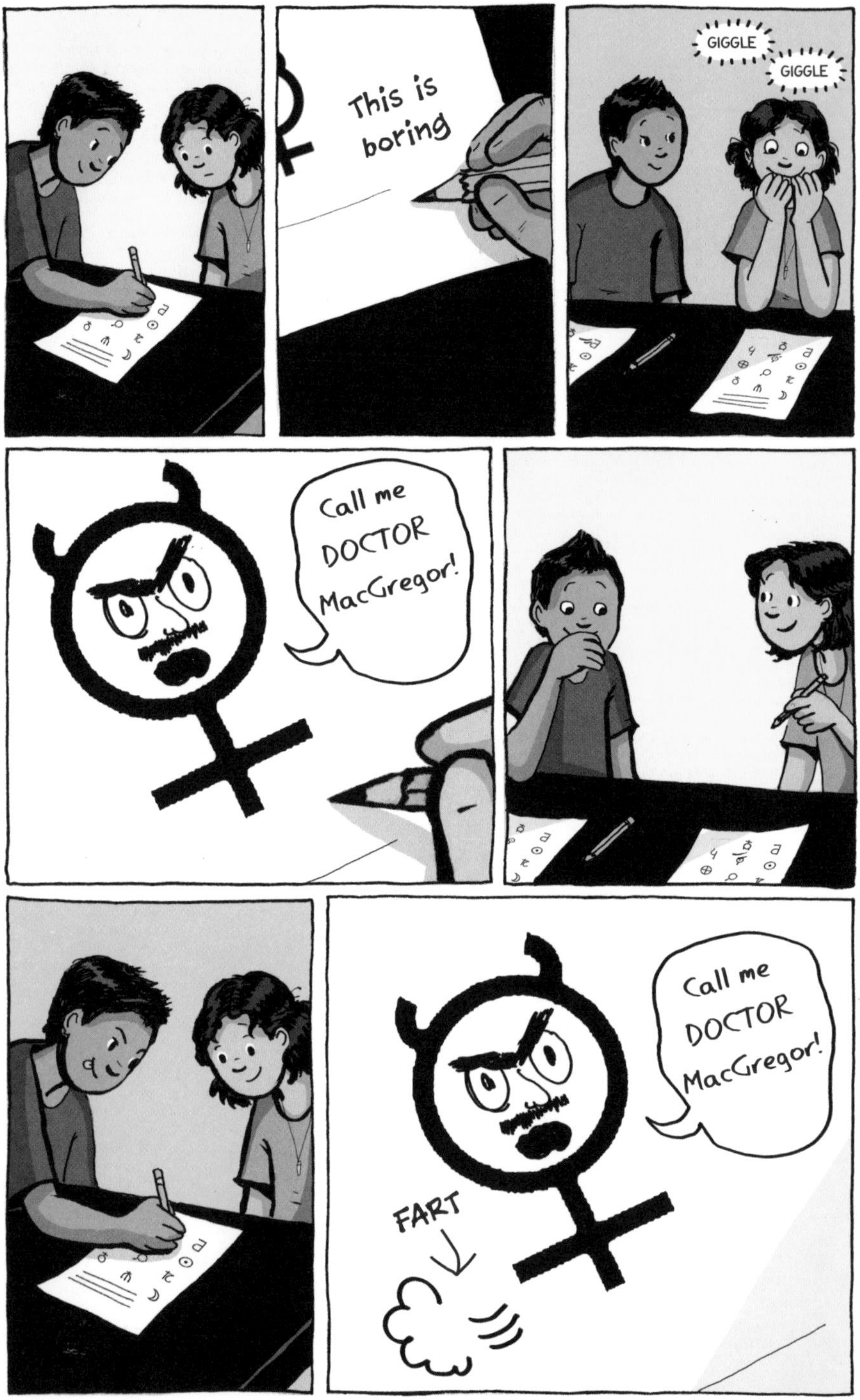
This is boring
GIGGLE
GIGGLE
Call me DOCTOR MacGregor!
Call me DOCTOR MacGregor!
FART

SNORT

THE CLASS WAS SO QUIET. SO VERY QUIET...

DON'T START LAUGHING. DON'T START LAUGHING.

BAAH-HA-HA-HA-HA-HA!!!

HA-HA-HA—HEH-HEH...

I SEE. SINCE YOU LOVEBIRDS CANNOT HANDLE SITTING NEXT TO EACH OTHER, WE ARE GOING TO HAVE TO SEPARATE YOU FOR THE REST OF THE CLASS. MS. VEGA, SWITCH PLACES WITH THE PERSON BEHIND YOU, PLEASE.

THE TWO OF YOU WILL EACH WRITE A PAPER ON A FAMOUS ASTRONOMER AND PRESENT IT TO THE CLASS IN THREE WEEKS' TIME. MR. KUO, YOU WILL PRESENT GALILEO GALILEI; MS. VEGA, YOU WILL PRESENT NICOLAUS COPERNICUS.

FOR THE REST OF CLASS—SILENT READING OF CHAPTER FIVE. TAKE NOTES ON WHAT YOU READ, AS THIS WILL BE ON OUR QUIZ ON MONDAY.

I TOOK NOTES IN CLASS, JUST LIKE HE ASKED. IMPORTANT NOTES. PROBABLY THE BEST NOTES I EVER TOOK, IN FACT.

AT LUNCH, IT FELT LIKE THE FIRST DAY OF SCHOOL ALL OVER AGAIN. I DIDN'T KNOW IF I SHOULD SIT AT MIKA'S TABLE OR NOT. SHE WAS STILL GIVING ME WEIRD LOOKS. FOR ABOUT THE 100TH TIME TODAY, I WANTED TO SINK INTO THE FLOOR AND DISAPPEAR.

HEY! HOMESCHOOL! COME OVER HERE! YOU GUYS HAVE TO SEE THIS DRAWING SHE DID OF DOCTOR MACGREGOR.

IT'S NOTHING REALLY...

I PULLED MY JOURNAL OUT ANYWAY.

WHOA!

IT LOOKS **EXACTLY** LIKE HIM! AND I'VE BEEN CLOSE ENOUGH TO SMELL HIS BREATH, SO THAT'S ACCURATE.

OH MY GOSH, YOU'RE **SO** GOOD.

MAYBE...THIS WAS WORKING? MAYBE EVERYONE DIDN'T HATE ME AFTER ALL!

LET ME SEE.

NO WAY. YOU DIDN'T DRAW THIS.

YES I **DID**.

OK. THEN DRAW SEÑORA SOSA.

OK.

DRAW MR. BOYD!

NOW DO MS. ARMSTRONG!

SHE'S LIKE A REAL CARTOONIST.

COME HERE—LOOK HOW GOOD SHE IS!

I HAVE TO ADMIT, IT FELT PRETTY GOOD TO BE THE CENTER OF ATTENTION IN A **GOOD** WAY.

DRAW MIKE LAWRENCE!

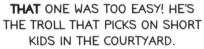

THAT ONE WAS TOO EASY! HE'S THE TROLL THAT PICKS ON SHORT KIDS IN THE COURTYARD.

NOW DO MITCHELL NGUYEN!

SEAN MILLER!

I GOT ONE. DO ANITA WALKER.

OH. UMM...ACTUALLY, I'M GOING TO EAT MY SANDWICH NOW. WE ONLY HAVE 5 MINUTES LEFT.

C'MON. IT'LL MAKE ME **SOOOO** HAPPY. PLEEEEEASE?

I FELT PRETTY BAD ABOUT THIS...BUT IT'S NOT LIKE SHE'D EVER SEE THE DRAWING.

Anita

NO, HER PANTS ARE HIGHER.

RRRRIIIIING!

I WALKED TO FIFTH PERIOD SURROUNDED BY PEOPLE...

SO WHY DID I FEEL SO ALONE?

USUALLY FAIRE HELPS ME FORGET ABOUT EVERYTHING ELSE. BUT I HAD A HARD TIME FORGETTING ABOUT MY PROBLEMS AT SCHOOL. EVERYTHING WAS GETTING SO DARK AND TWISTY AND **COMPLICATED**.

DOES MIKA LIKE ME? OR DOES SHE HATE ME? DO I EVEN **WANT** TO BE FRIENDS WITH HER? SHE INVITED ME TO SIT WITH HER ON THE FIRST DAY OF SCHOOL...**AND** TO HER HOUSE...**AND** HER BIRTHDAY PARTY. BUT **THEN** THERE WAS THAT WHOLE THING WITH THE SAMMIES...

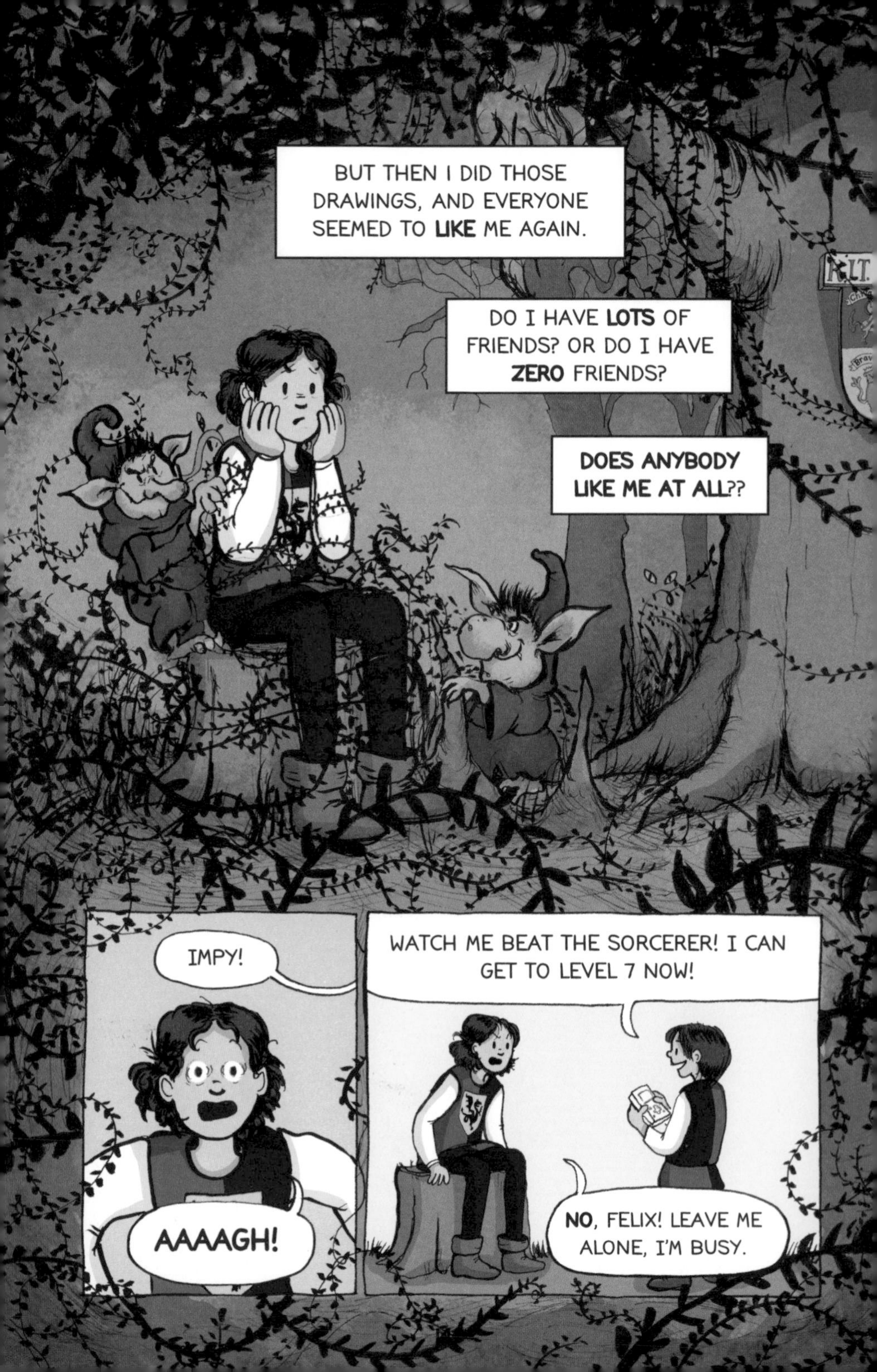
BUT THEN I DID THOSE DRAWINGS, AND EVERYONE SEEMED TO **LIKE** ME AGAIN.
DO I HAVE **LOTS** OF FRIENDS? OR DO I HAVE **ZERO** FRIENDS?
DOES ANYBODY LIKE ME AT ALL??
IMPY!
AAAAGH!
WATCH ME BEAT THE SORCERER! I CAN GET TO LEVEL 7 NOW!
NO, FELIX! LEAVE ME ALONE, I'M BUSY.

YOU'RE NO FUN! AND YOU'RE NOT BUSY, YOU'RE JUST SITTING THERE!

GO **AWAY**, FELIX!

RRRRRRAAAGH!

RRRRRRRRGH!! **SO ANNOYING!**

GOOD MORROW, IMOGENE.

OH YEAH, AND NOT TO MENTION, I STILL FELT GUILTY ABOUT THAT DRAWING OF ANITA. EVEN IF SHE'D NEVER SEE IT, IT WAS STILL MEAN. WHY DID I LET MIKA MAKE ME DO IT?

THE MORNING SESSION OF K.I.T. WENT SLOOOOOWWLY, EVEN THOUGH ANITA WAS IN A GOOD MOOD.

NOW PARRY LEFT, AND ...YES, YOU'VE GOT IT! WELL DONE, FELIX!

FINALLY IT WAS NOON, AND TIME FOR THE PARADE. MAYBE THE DISTRACTION WOULD KEEP ME FROM FEELING GUILTY/NERVOUS/BARFY FOR A LITTLE WHILE.

THE PARADE LEADS RIGHT TO THE CHESS FIELD—SO EVERYONE WILL STAY AND WATCH THE MATCH. I SETTLED ON MY USUAL SQUARE AND WAITED FOR THE QUEEN TO START THE SHOW.

BEGGING YOUR PARDON, LADY IMOGENE.

YOU MAY KNOW OF ME—I AM ANITA'S FATHER.

OH. HELLO. I MEAN, GOOD DAY, SIR.

I WANTED TO THANK YOU, YOUNG LADY. IT'S BEEN A WHILE SINCE ANITA'S SPOKEN OF ANY FRIENDS—I'M HAPPY TO SEE SHE HAS FINALLY MADE A FRIEND HER OWN AGE.

OH MAN. WHAT ARE YOU SUPPOSED TO SAY WHEN GROWN-UPS TELL YOU SOMETHING EMBARRASSING ABOUT THEIR KIDS?

UM...

I SHALL LEAVE YE TO YOUR DUTIES, BUT THANK YOU FOR MAKING MY DAUGHTER HAPPY. YOU DO SERVICE TO YOUR FAMILY AND YOUR KINGDOM.

AND I THOUGHT I COULDN'T FEEL ANY WORSE. I FELT BAD ALL DAY...

AND I HAD A HARD TIME FALLING ASLEEP THAT NIGHT.

STILL NO STARS.

143

I WAS SO NERVOUS ABOUT GOING BACK TO SCHOOL ON MONDAY THAT I COULDN'T ENJOY FAIRE AT ALL ON SUNDAY.

OI! IMPY! I ASKED IF YE WANTED AN APPLE DUMPLING!

NO THANKS. I'M NOT HUNGRY.

OH NO. YE HAVEN'T GOT THE PLAGUE, HAVE YE? QUICK, GET THE LEECHES!

IT'S NOTHING, IT'S...

WELL, THERE'S THIS GIRL AT SCHOOL.

HANG ON.

LET'S GET COMFORTABLE.

ALL RIGHT, GO ON—THERE'S THIS GIRL AT SCHOOL...

WELL, SHE KIND OF TELLS EVERYONE WHAT TO DO. AND SOMETIMES SHE'S NICE, BUT SOMETIMES SHE'S NOT. AND OTHER TIMES, SHE MAKES...OTHER PEOPLE...DO NOT-SO-NICE THINGS.

WELL, WHY DON'T YOU STAND UP TO HER? TELL HER SHE'S BEING A NINCOMPOOP AND TO CUT IT OUT.

MIKA, THOU ART A NINCOMPOOP.

HA!

HA!

ADULTS GIVE **THE WORST** ADVICE SOMETIMES.

IF I STAND UP TO HER, I WON'T HAVE ANY FRIENDS AT ALL. I DON'T KNOW WHAT TO DO.

WELL, SHE SOUNDS LIKE A RIGHT BULLY TO ME, AND SHE'S NOT WORTH YOUR TIME.

SIGH

OI! SIR GEORGE! WHAT DOES A GREAT KNIGHT LIKE YOURSELF DO WHEN YE COME ACROSS A BULLY?

A BULLY, EH? I'LL TELL YE WHAT I DO TO BULLIES...

145

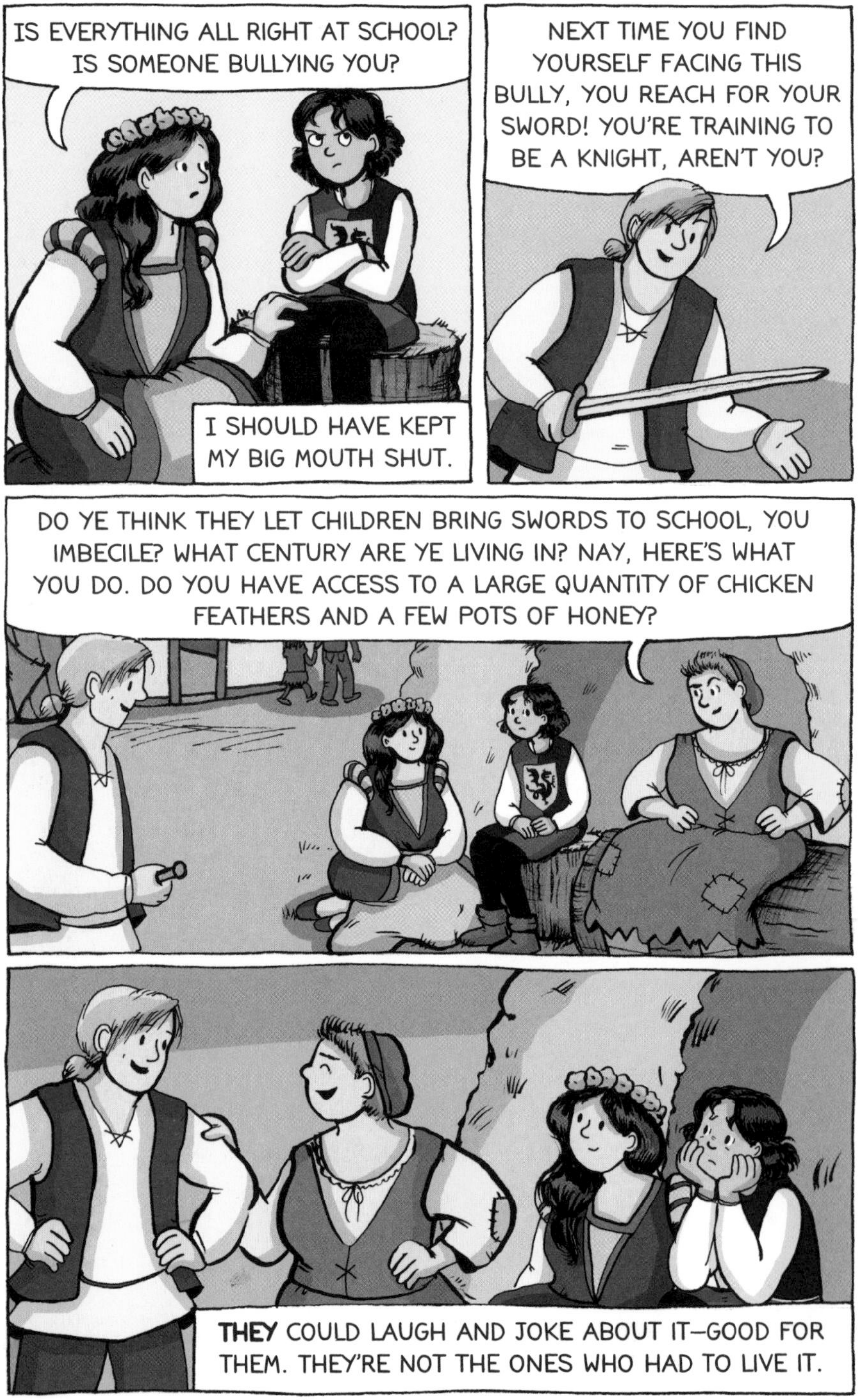
IS EVERYTHING ALL RIGHT AT SCHOOL? IS SOMEONE BULLYING YOU?
I SHOULD HAVE KEPT MY BIG MOUTH SHUT.
NEXT TIME YOU FIND YOURSELF FACING THIS BULLY, YOU REACH FOR YOUR SWORD! YOU'RE TRAINING TO BE A KNIGHT, AREN'T YOU?
DO YE THINK THEY LET CHILDREN BRING SWORDS TO SCHOOL, YOU IMBECILE? WHAT CENTURY ARE YE LIVING IN? NAY, HERE'S WHAT YOU DO. DO YOU HAVE ACCESS TO A LARGE QUANTITY OF CHICKEN FEATHERS AND A FEW POTS OF HONEY?
THEY COULD LAUGH AND JOKE ABOUT IT—GOOD FOR THEM. THEY'RE NOT THE ONES WHO HAD TO LIVE IT.

CHAPTER EIGHT

Every knight in shining armor must face trials and tribulations on her quest toward enlightenment. Unfortunately, our hero is about to face some serious trials and tribulations. In fact, it may just be the worst week of her entire life. Dost thou not believe me? Here is a day-by-day account.

Monday

AS I GOT READY FOR SCHOOL, I THOUGHT ABOUT THE ADVICE EVERYONE GAVE. DON'T PAY ATTENTION TO BULLIES. JUST BE YOURSELF.

HOW DO I KNOW WHO "MYSELF" IS? I'VE NEVER GONE TO MIDDLE SCHOOL BEFORE!

I DON'T HAVE ANYTHING TO **WEAR**!

ADULTS ALWAYS TELL YOU NOT TO CARE ABOUT WHAT OTHER PEOPLE THINK ABOUT YOU. THAT'S EASY FOR **THEM** TO SAY, BECAUSE THEY'RE NOT IN MIDDLE SCHOOL.

KICK

I SAW WHAT HAPPENED TO KIDS WHO DIDN'T HAVE ANY FRIENDS.

HEY, IMOGENE! DID YOU DO ANY NEW DRAWINGS THIS WEEKEND?

SOME PEOPLE STILL LIKE ME. I WAS HANGING ON BY A THREAD, BUT I COULD STILL FIX THIS...I COULD TRY TO START OVER. IT WAS WORTH A SHOT.

I USED CLASS TIME TO TAKE IMPORTANT NOTES FOR MY NEW PLAN.

I'D START WITH COSTUMING. AFTER FOUR WEEKS OF WORK, I HAD EIGHTY DOLLARS. THAT SHOULD BUY ME A LOT OF STUFF.

Clothes List

1. Sammies
2. Jeans with heart on pocket
3. Flower headbands
4. Shirt with puffy sleeves

CLASS, FIVE MINUTES REMAINING FOR YOUR QUIZ.

OH, FIE!

A, B, C, D. A, B, C, D. DONE.

AFTER SCHOOL, I WROTE OUT A LIST OF VERY CONVINCING ARGUMENTS AND DID A QUICK MENTAL CALCULATION.

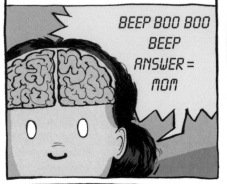

BEEP BOO BOO BEEP ANSWER = MOM

I PRESENTED MY CASE AS SOON AS SHE GOT HOME.

MOM!

AGHHHHHH!

I NEED YOU TO TAKE ME TO THE MALL. HERE ARE MY REASONS.

ONE: I WILL USE MY OWN MONEY, SO YOU DON'T NEED TO PAY FOR ANYTHING.

TWO: I NEED SOME NEW JEANS AND SHIRTS. IT GETS VERY COLD IN MY CLASSROOMS.

THREE: I NEED SOME MORE FASHIONABLE CLOTHES. I KNOW IT'S BEEN A LONG TIME SINCE **YOU'VE** BEEN IN SCHOOL, BUT THIS ISN'T REALLY WHAT KIDS ARE WEARING THESE DAYS.

FOUR...

IMPY! IT'S OK! I'M NOT **THAT** ANCIENT THAT I DON'T REMEMBER WHAT MIDDLE SCHOOL IS LIKE. WE CAN GO TO THE MALL.

YAY! I'LL GO GET DAD AND FELIX!

YOU KNOW WHAT? LET'S MAKE IT A GIRLS' TRIP. JUST YOU AND ME.

REALLY? OK!

USUALLY FELIX REQUIRES, WELL, A BIT OF ATTENTION...SO IT WASN'T THAT OFTEN THAT I GOT TO GO PLACES ALONE WITH MOM.

IT WAS KIND OF NICE!

WE GOT CINNAMON SUGAR SOFT PRETZELS, WHICH ARE, IN MY OPINION, THE MOST DELICIOUS FOOD IN THE WORLD.

MMMMMMMM!

MOM TOLD ME STORIES ABOUT HER SIXTH-GRADE BOYFRIEND.

DANIEL BOYD! HE HAD THE NICEST GREEN EYES...

MOM! YOU'RE A MARRIED WOMAN!

OH PLEASE. THIS WAS THIRTY YEARS AGO. YOUR FATHER HAS NOTHING TO WORRY ABOUT.

WHAT IF YOU HAD **MARRIED** DANIEL BOYD? WHAT WOULD HAVE HAPPENED THEN?

YOU'D PROBABLY HAVE GREEN EYES AND WOULD BE LIVING IN MINNESOTA.

WHOA... WEIRD.

I WAS JUST RELAXING INTO A COMFY POST-PRETZEL STATE WHEN MOM POUNCED.

SWALLOW

SPEAKING OF BOYFRIENDS...I WANT TO TALK TO YOU ABOUT SOMETHING.

NOW, I WASN'T **SNOOPING**, BUT I WAS PUTTING SOME THINGS AWAY IN YOUR ROOM AND I SAW...A BOOK.

Summer Love

OH, FIE!

I WANT YOU TO KNOW, IT'S PERFECTLY NORMAL TO BE CURIOUS ABOUT THESE THINGS AT YOUR AGE, AND...

BUT IT'S NOT MY BOOK! IT'S **MIKA'S** BOOK! SHE JUST PUT IT IN MY BACKPACK BY MISTAKE!

MIKA—SHE'S THE GIRL WHOSE HOUSE YOU WENT TO LAST WEEK? I SHOULD MEET HER, TALK TO HER PARENTS...IS SHE FRIENDS WITH ANITA TOO? ARE THE THREE OF YOU FRIENDS AT SCHOOL?

OH, IF ONLY SHE KNEW.

MY **POINT** IS, SOMETIMES KIDS HAVE WRONG INFORMATION ABOUT SEX...

MOM!

...AND IF YOU WANT TO KNOW ANYTHING, YOU CAN COME TO ME. OK?

TIP

OK! CAN WE GO NOW? **PLEASE**?

IF I NEVER HEAR MY MOM SAY THE WORD "SEX" AGAIN, I CAN DIE HAPPY.

15 % OFF

I TRIED TO LOSE MYSELF IN THE SPINNING RACKS OF DENIM RIGHT QUICK.

I HAD EIGHTY DOLLARS TO SPEND AND I WAS READY TO USE IT. I CONSULTED MY LIST. JEANS WITH A LITTLE HEART SEWN ON THE BACK POCKET...

OH, HERE ARE THEY ARE...

$110?!? WHAT?!

$80...$65...$75...I CAN'T AFFORD ANY OF THIS STUFF!

...MOM? COULD YOU...?

IMPY...I DON'T MIND BUYING YOU CLOTHES. BUT $110 FOR A PAIR OF JEANS IS A LITTLE RIDICULOUS. ESPECIALLY SINCE YOU'LL GROW OUT OF THEM IN SIX MONTHS ANYWAY.

I KNOW.

I **DID** KNOW IT WAS RIDICULOUS. THAT THE KIND OF JEANS I WORE DIDN'T MATTER. THAT I SHOULDN'T CARE WHAT ANYONE THOUGHT ABOUT MY CLOTHES.

BUT I STILL **WANTED THOSE JEANS**.

I HAVE AN IDEA. COME ON.

THE THRIFT STORE?

Eagle Thrift

JUST COME AND TAKE A LOOK. TRUST ME.

IT SMELLED FUNNY IN THIS STORE. AND IT WAS DARK, AND NOT NEARLY AS FUN AS THE MALL. UNTIL...

AREN'T THESE THE KIND OF JEANS YOU WERE LOOKING AT? THEY'RE YOUR SIZE.

YEAH...SIX BUCKS?!?

LOOKS LIKE THERE'S A LITTLE BIT OF PAINT ON THE LEG THERE...

I DIDN'T CARE. AT SIX DOLLARS, I COULD DEAL WITH SOME PAINT. I'D BE THE BEST-DRESSED KID AT SCHOOL!

I LOADED UP ON STUFF I RECOGNIZED FROM MY RESEARCH. I EVEN FOUND A **REAL** PAIR OF SAMMIES.

$16.42 IS YOUR CHANGE.

Thank You

SO? WAS I RIGHT, OR WAS I RIGHT?

NUDGE

I GUESS... THANKS, MOM.

EVERYONE SAID I WAS JUST LIKE MY DAD. BUT SOMETIMES...**SOMETIMES**, MOM UNDERSTOOD THINGS PRETTY WELL TOO.

Tuesday

KNOCK
KNOCK

IMOGENE? YOUR BROTHER NEEDS THE BATHROOM. DID YOU SEE THE LAUNDRY PILE I LEFT BY YOUR DOOR? I WASHED YOUR NEW CLOTHES LAST NIGHT.

I SAW! BE RIGHT OUT!

HERE GOES NOTHING...

THAT'S A NEW LOOK FOR YOU. ARE YOU GOING FOR PREP SCHOOL DROPOUT?

HUSH, HUGO. I THINK YOU LOOK VERY NICE, IMOGENE.

THANK YOU, MOTHER. IT'S A LOOK I CALL "NORMAL PERSON WHO COMES FROM A NORMAL FAMILY."

ANYWAY.... CATCH YOU LATER!

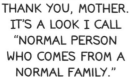

NEW OUTFIT: SO FAR, SO GOOD.

LET'S SEE MIKA SAY ANYTHING ABOUT MY CLOTHES **NOW!**

GOOD MORNING, MIKA.

HEY, IMOGENE. NEW OUTFIT?

YES, AS A MATTER OF FACT, IT IS!

I DON'T REALLY KNOW HOW TO SAY THIS, BUT...IT'S NOT TOO COOL TO COPY SOMEONE ELSE'S CLOTHES.

WHAT?

YOU'RE DRESSED PRETTY MUCH EXACTLY LIKE ME AND EMILY. YOU DON'T HAVE TO **COPY** PEOPLE.

FOR WEEKS NOW, I'VE BEEN QUIET, AND NERVOUS, AND SCARED AROUND MIKA. I TRIED TO DO EVERYTHING RIGHT, AND IT **STILL** WASN'T GOOD ENOUGH.

AND MAYBE IT WAS A BAD IDEA, BUT I'D JUST ABOUT HAD IT WITH MIKA AND HER RULES. I COULDN'T STOP MYSELF.

I STOOD UP TO THE DRAGON.

SO **FIRST** YOU MAKE FUN OF ME BECAUSE I'M NOT WEARING THE SAME CLOTHES AS EVERYONE ELSE. **THEN** YOU MAKE FUN OF ME BECAUSE I **AM** WEARING THE SAME CLOTHES AS EVERYONE ELSE. WHICH ONE IS IT?

OOOOOOOOOOOOOO!

I'M JUST **SAYING**, YOU SHOULD FIND YOUR OWN STYLE. YOU SHOULDN'T COPY SOMEONE ELSE TO TRY AND LOOK COOL.

LIKE THOSE JEANS. **EVERYONE** WEARS THAT BRAND OF JEANS. I HAD A PAIR LAST YEAR, BUT WE DONATED THEM TO CHARITY WHEN I SPILLED SOME PAINT ON THEM.

UH-OH.

ACTUALLY...I HAD A PAIR **EXACTLY** LIKE THOSE. WHERE DID YOU GET THOSE JEANS?

AT...AT THE MALL

I SPILLED PAINT ON THE LEG THAT LOOKS LIKE FLORIDA. LET ME SEE YOUR LEG.

I SEE FLORIDA! I SEE FLORIDA!

ARE YOU **ACTUALLY** WEARING MY OLD JEANS? THE ONES I GAVE AWAY TO **CHARITY**? ARE YOU POOR OR SOMETHING?

NO!

I CAN'T BELIEVE YOU'RE WEARING MY OLD JEANS. EWW, I FEEL SO DIRTY! THAT'S SO GROSS. LET ME CHECK AND MAKE SURE...

GET AWAY FROM ME! GET **AWAY**!

OW! YOU KICKED MY FACE WITH YOUR STUPID CHARITY SNEAKERS!

...AAAAAAAND YEP. I'M DEAD.

I'D NEVER LIVE THIS DOWN. NEVER. EVER. EVER. EVER.

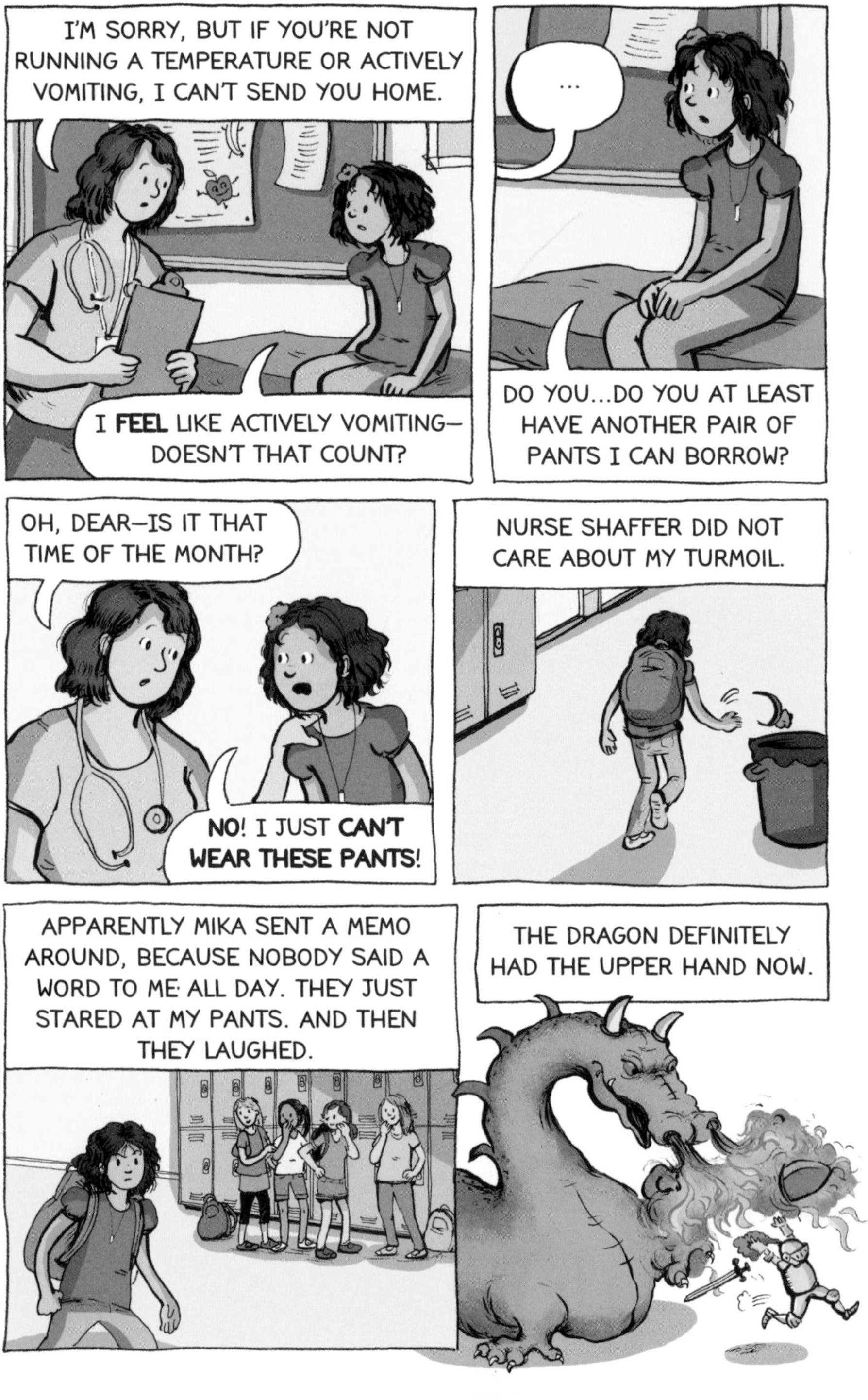
I'M SORRY, BUT IF YOU'RE NOT RUNNING A TEMPERATURE OR ACTIVELY VOMITING, I CAN'T SEND YOU HOME.
I **FEEL** LIKE ACTIVELY VOMITING—DOESN'T THAT COUNT?
...
DO YOU...DO YOU AT LEAST HAVE ANOTHER PAIR OF PANTS I CAN BORROW?
OH, DEAR—IS IT THAT TIME OF THE MONTH?
NO! I JUST **CAN'T WEAR THESE PANTS**!
NURSE SHAFFER DID NOT CARE ABOUT MY TURMOIL.
APPARENTLY MIKA SENT A MEMO AROUND, BECAUSE NOBODY SAID A WORD TO ME ALL DAY. THEY JUST STARED AT MY PANTS. AND THEN THEY LAUGHED.
THE DRAGON DEFINITELY HAD THE UPPER HAND NOW.

SOMEHOW I MADE IT THROUGH THE END OF THE DAY...

AND THE BUS RIDE...

AND THE WALK HOME.

SLAM!

AH! THAT MUST BE THE DULCET TONES OF MY GENTLE DAUGHTER RETURNING HOME.

SO? WERE THE NEW CLOTHES A HIT? DID EVERYONE LOVE THE NEW "PREP SCHOOL DROPOUT" LOOK?

EVERYTHING'S A JOKE TO YOU! IT'S NOT **FUNNY**!

IMOGENE, WHAT'S WRONG? WHAT HAPPENED?

EVERYONE **KNEW** THEY WERE SECONDHAND CLOTHES. THEY SAID WE WERE POOR.

OH, HONEY. COME HERE.

WELL, THEY'RE NOT WRONG THERE—WE ARE POOR.

I **TOLD** YOU, IT'S NOT FUNNY! WHY CAN'T YOU JUST HAVE NORMAL JOBS, SO WE CAN BUY CLOTHES AT NORMAL STORES LIKE NORMAL PEOPLE?

WELL, WHEN YOU GROW UP, YOU CAN HAVE WHATEVER NORMAL JOB YOU WANT.

YEP, YOU CAN BE A DENTIST, OR A LAWYER, OR...OOH, AN ACCOUNTANT! YOU COULD DO OUR TAXES FOR US!

HA! HA!

YOU DON'T KNOW ANYTHING ABOUT REAL JOBS! YOU DON'T HAVE A REAL JOB! YOU'RE A POOL BOY.

HEY. COOL IT, IMOGENE.

WE DON'T EVEN HAVE A REAL HOUSE—WE LIVE IN THIS STUPID APARTMENT...

THAT'S ENOUGH, IMOGENE.

WITH A STUPID CAR THAT DOESN'T EVEN RUN HALF THE TIME. AND YOU'RE NOT A REAL ACTOR ANYWAY, IT'S JUST A STUPID FAIRE THAT DOESN'T MEAN—

IMOGENE. TO YOUR ROOM. NOW.

FINE!

SLAM!

IT'S ALL FINE AND WELL FOR MY PARENTS TO LIVE IN A FANTASY WORLD. BUT THEY SHOULDN'T FORCE ME INTO IT TOO.

APPARENTLY MY FAMILY WAS GIVING ME THE SILENT TREATMENT, BECAUSE MY MOM ONLY SAID FOUR WORDS TO ME THE NEXT MORNING.

I'M NOT GOING TO SCHOOL TODAY.

OH. YES. YOU. ARE.

OH YES I DID.

SCHOOL BUS STOP

NO ONE SAID ANYTHING TO ME AT SCHOOL. ONLY ANITA LOOKED AT ME, AND I COULD READ THAT SMIRK AS CLEAR AS A BOOK.

"I TOLD YOU THOSE KIDS WERE NOT YOUR FRIENDS."

MY FIRST PERSONAL INTERACTION OF THE DAY TOOK PLACE IN SCIENCE CLASS, SO YOU KNOW IT WASN'T GOOD.

I WAS PUTTING MY "SIGNED" TEST IN *THE DOCTOR'S* BOX. I HAD TO KEEP FORGING THE SIGNATURE—I COULDN'T CHANGE IT **NOW**. WHEN I GOT BACK TO MY SEAT...

PEOPLE, PLEASE PULL OUT YOUR TEXTBOOKS AND TURN TO PAGE 88.

164

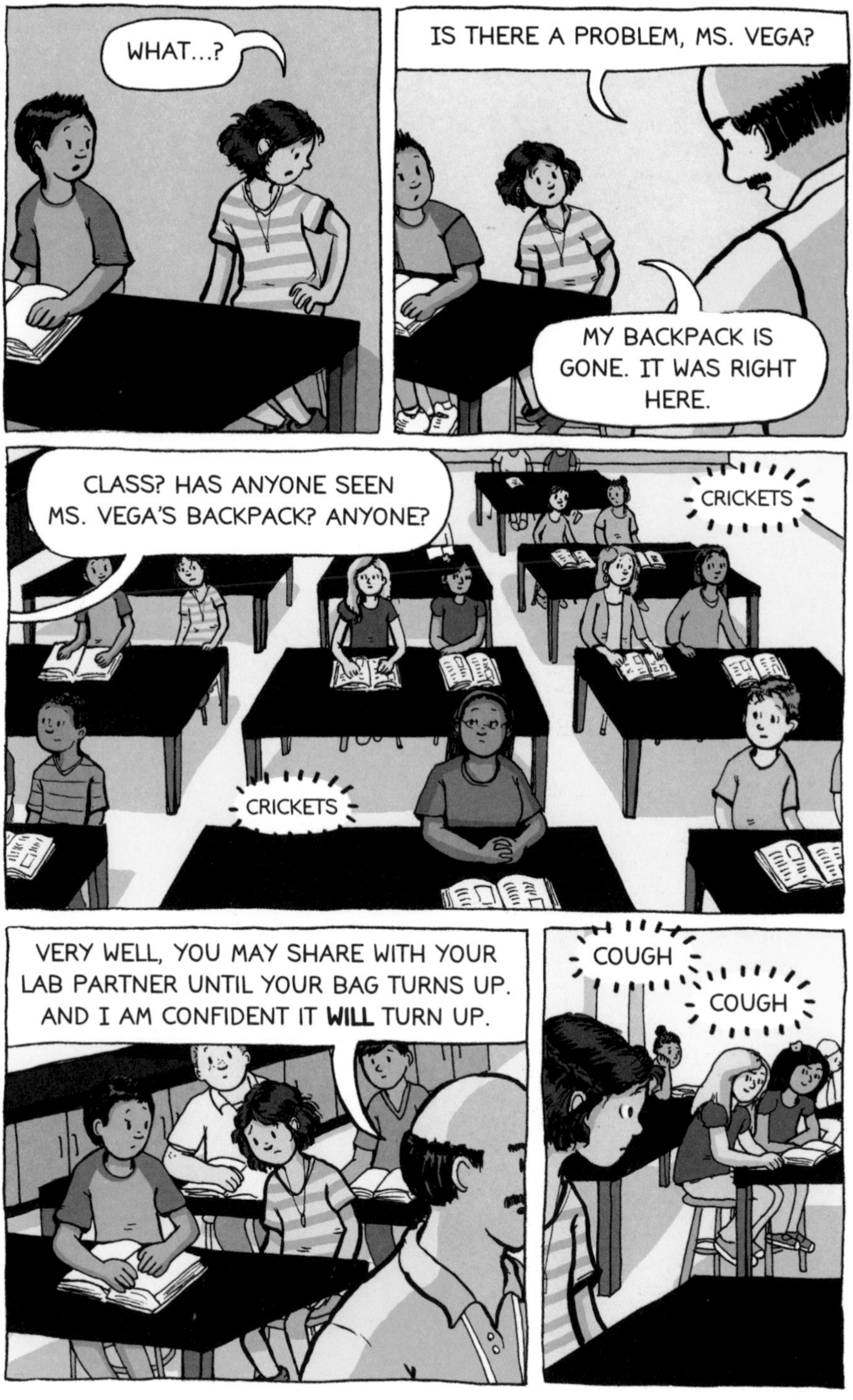
WHAT...?
IS THERE A PROBLEM, MS. VEGA?
MY BACKPACK IS GONE. IT WAS RIGHT HERE.
CLASS? HAS ANYONE SEEN MS. VEGA'S BACKPACK? ANYONE?
CRICKETS
CRICKETS
VERY WELL, YOU MAY SHARE WITH YOUR LAB PARTNER UNTIL YOUR BAG TURNS UP. AND I AM CONFIDENT IT **WILL** TURN UP.
COUGH
COUGH

THE GOOD NEWS WAS: I FOUND MY BACKPACK AFTER CLASS.

THE BAD NEWS?

CALENDAR, BINDER, PENCIL CASE...I THINK THAT'S EVERYTH...

OH NO.

I FELT LIKE ACTIVELY VOMITING.

MY JOURNAL WAS MISSING.

Thursday

...ACTUALLY, NOTHING ESPECIALLY BAD HAPPENED TODAY, BESIDES GETTING IGNORED. BUT FRIDAY WOULD MAKE UP FOR IT.

Friday

IT TOOK A FEW MINUTES FOR WHAT I SAW IN THE SIXTH-GRADE HALLWAY THAT MORNING TO SINK IN.

ANITA, I...

MS. VEGA, YOU'RE WANTED IN THE VICE PRINCIPAL'S OFFICE.

AND I'D KEEP YOUR DAY JOB, BY THE WAY—THIS LOOKS NOTHING LIKE ME.

I TRIED NOT TO CRY AS I SAT IN THE HARD PLASTIC CHAIRS. I TRIED NOT TO CRY AS I HEARD THE SECRETARY CALL MY PARENTS.

I TRIED NOT TO CRY AS WE WAITED TO BE CALLED IN.

IMPY, WHY WON'T YOU TELL US WHAT'S GOING ON?

MR. AND MRS. VEGA. IMOGENE. PLEASE COME IN.

MRS. STONE, **WHAT** IS THIS ALL ABOUT?

Hang in

There!

I'M AFRAID WE HAVE AN INSTANCE OF BULLYING ON OUR HANDS, AND OUR SCHOOL HAS A ZERO TOLERANCE POLICY FOR BULLYING.

OH, NO. I FEEL TERRIBLE. I KNEW SOME KIDS HAD BEEN PICKING ON IMP—IMOGENE BECAUSE OF HER CLOTHES, BUT I DIDN'T REALIZE IT WAS THIS BAD. ARE THE KIDS WHO HAVE BEEN BULLYING HER GOING TO GET REPRIMANDED?

I'M AFRAID YOU DON'T UNDERSTAND. **YOUR DAUGHTER** IS THE ONE DOING THE BULLYING.

IMOGENE? NO. THERE MUST BE SOME MISTAKE.

WE FOUND THESE DRAWINGS IN THE SIXTH-GRADE WING THIS MORNING.

DID YOU **DRAW** THESE, IMOGENE?

WHAT ELSE COULD I SAY?

YES.

BUT I DIDN'T TAPE THEM TO ANYONE'S LOCKER! SOMEBODY **ELSE** DID THAT TO BE MEAN TO **ME**!

MOM KEPT FLIPPING THROUGH THE DRAWINGS LIKE SHE COULDN'T BELIEVE WHAT SHE WAS SEEING. I WANTED TO RIP THEM INTO A THOUSAND PIECES.

THESE ARE REALLY MEAN, IMOGENE. I'VE NEVER KNOWN YOU TO BE **MEAN**. I DON'T UNDERSTAND...IS THIS ANITA? I THOUGHT SHE WAS YOUR **FRIEND**.

NOW, WE ARE AWARE THAT IMOGENE HAS BEEN HAVING A TOUGH TIME ADJUSTING TO SCHOOL. AS YOU KNOW, SHE CURRENTLY HAS A FAILING GRADE IN SCIENCE...

PARDON ME?

WE HAVE HER SIGNED TESTS FROM YOU RIGHT HERE.

WE DIDN'T SIGN THESE TESTS.

THERE WAS A STRANGE STILLNESS IN THE ROOM, LIKE RIGHT BEFORE A THUNDERSTORM.

IMOGENE, CAN YOU EXPLAIN TO US **WHAT** IS GOING ON?

I COULDN'T TALK—I THOUGHT I WOULD CHOKE. I JUST SHOOK MY HEAD AND WAITED FOR IT TO BE OVER.

I WAITED TO HEAR THE VICE PRINCIPAL SAY I WAS SUSPENDED FROM SCHOOL FOR THREE DAYS.

WAITED FOR MOM AND DAD TO DRIVE ME HOME.

THANKS FOR WATCHING HIM ON SUCH SHORT NOTICE, VERNA.

WHAT'S GOING ON?

WAITED TO BE LEFT ALONE IN MY ROOM.

DID SOMEONE **MAKE** YOU DO THOSE DRAWINGS, KIDDO?

WE JUST WANT TO KNOW WHAT'S GOING ON, SWEETIE.

THEY LOOKED SO CONFUSED AND...**DISAPPOINTED**.

I DIDN'T **MEAN** TO BE MEAN.

HOW COULD I EXPLAIN WHAT HAD HAPPENED... WHEN I DIDN'T REALLY UNDERSTAND IT MYSELF?

WHAT'S HAPPENING? WHY IS IMPY CRYING?

YOUR SISTER HAS SOME THINKING TO DO. LET'S LEAVE HER ALONE FOR A WHILE.

I COULD HEAR MY PARENTS TALKING IN THE KITCHEN AFTER THAT. IT STARTED TO GET DARK, BUT NOBODY CAME TO GET ME FOR DINNER.

IMPY? YOU CAN PLAY MY VIDEO GAME IF YOU WANT.

I WISH I HAD A DOG—A DOG WOULD STILL LOVE ME.

INSTEAD, I JUST LAY THERE STARING AT THE STARLESS SKY AND TRIED TO FALL ASLEEP.

CHAPTER NINE

When a knight in shining armor is at a low point in their journey and all seems lost, the only way to go is...even lower. Aye, thou hast heard me correctly—Imogene's week is about to get EVEN WORSE.

I COULD TELL MOM AND DAD HAD TALKED ABOUT WHAT TO DO WITH ME ON SATURDAY MORNING. THEY DIDN'T WANT TO REWARD ME BY LETTING ME GO TO FAIRE, BUT THEY COULDN'T LET ME STAY HOME BY MYSELF, EITHER.

UNTIL YOU'RE READY TO TALK TO US AND TELL US WHAT'S GOING ON, WE'RE TAKING AWAY YOUR SQUIRE PRIVILEGES. **AND** YOUR COSTUME.

WHAT AM I GOING TO DO INSTEAD?

YOU'LL STAY IN THE STORE WITH ME AND HELP WATCH FELIX. JUST LIKE BEFORE. YOU HAVE TO **PROVE** TO US YOU ARE MATURE ENOUGH TO RESUME YOUR SQUIRE DUTIES.

WHEN WE GOT TO FAIRE, I SAT IN THE BACK AND WORKED THE CASH BOX—THE JOB THAT REQUIRED THE LEAST AMOUNT OF EFFORT AND HUMAN INTERACTION.

BONUS: I DIDN'T HAVE TO WALK AROUND AND POSSIBLY RUN INTO ANITA.

NOBODY SAID ANYTHING TO ME (EXCEPT FOR THE PRINCESS).

GOOD DAY, IMOGENE!

IT'S WHAT I DESERVED.

AFTER A FULL DAY OF SAYING NOTHING BUT "HERE IS THY CHANGE" AND "WOULD THOU LIKEST A BAG FOR THY PURCHASE?"...

WHO, MOI??

FINE.

IMOGENE, TAKE YOUR BROTHER TO THE PRIVIES, PLEASE. HE IS DRIVING ME INSANE.

IT'S LIKE THE PEOPLE ENJOYING THEMSELVES AROUND ME WERE IN A DIFFERENT WORLD. THOUGHTS OF SCHOOL HUNG OVER MY HEAD LIKE A DARK CLOUD AND PUT EVERYTHING ELSE IN SHADOWS. PLUS, ANITA COULD SHOW UP AROUND ANY CORNER.

HERE, HOLD TIFFANY WHILE I GO!

WHENEVER I THOUGHT ABOUT MY JOURNAL, I GOT A SICK FEELING IN THE PIT OF MY STOMACH.

WHY DID I MAKE THAT DRAWING? **WHY** DIDN'T I RIP IT UP?

I HAD TO GET AWAY AND BE ALONE FOR A SECOND.

RUSTLE

RUSTLE

KISS

WHAT IS **HAPPENING**? WHY IS EVERYTHING CHANGING? WHY CAN'T THINGS GO BACK TO THE WAY THEY WERE?

IMPY? **IMPY!** WHERE ARE YOU?

JUST FIVE MORE MINUTES OF SOLITUDE. FIVE MORE MINUTES...

WAKEY WAKEY!

SHOVE

I GOT YOU! HA-HA! NOW **YOU** FELL IN THE MUD PIT!

NOW GIVE ME TIFFANY BACK.

THAT'S IT. I'VE HAD IT. I'VE HAD IT WITH **YOU**, I'VE HAD IT WITH THIS **STUPID** FAIRE, AND MY WHOLE **STUPID LIFE**. YOU WANT TIFFANY BACK?

GO GET HER.

FLING

HAVE YOU EVER DONE SOMETHING, THEN INSTANTLY REGRETTED IT?

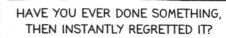

SPLASH

TIFFANY?!

NO! FELIX, DON'T GO IN THERE!

LET ME GO! SHE'S SINKING! SHE'S SINKING INTO THE LAKE!

KICK

KICK

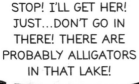

STOP! I'LL GET HER! JUST...DON'T GO IN THERE! THERE ARE PROBABLY ALLIGATORS IN THAT LAKE!

THE ALLIGATORS ARE GONNA EEEAA-A-A-T TIFFANY!

WAAAAAAAAAAAA!

JUST...HANG ON.

YOU'RE PUSHING HER FARTHER OUT!

WHAT'S GOING ON? WHAT'S HAPPENING?

TIFFANY FELL IN THE LAKE AND SHE'S DROWNING!

I'M TRYING TO GET HER BACK BUT I CAN'T REACH HER!

IMOGENE, DON'T GO ANY FARTHER OUT ON THAT BRANCH. I'M GOING TO GET THE GROUNDSKEEPER. FELIX, YOU STAY PUT.

TIFFANY!

IT'S OK, FELIX. WE'LL GET HER OUT.

THINGS WERE PRETTY CHAOTIC AFTER THAT. IT SEEMED LIKE THE WHOLE FAIRE CAME OUT TO TRY AND FIND TIFFANY.

BY NIGHTTIME, IT WAS PRETTY CLEAR WE WOULDN'T FIND HER TODAY.

WELL, IT'S A MAN-MADE LAKE, AND IT DRAINS OUT TO THE GULF OF MEXICO...

MEXICOOOOOOOOOOOO!!!

I SHALL SET MY ENTIRE ROYAL GUARD ON LOOKOUT!

WE'LL COME BACK FIRST THING TOMORROW WHEN IT'S LIGHT OUT—MAYBE SHE'LL WASH ASHORE OVERNIGHT.

BUT SHE'LL BE COLD AND WET! I CAN'T JUST LEAVE HER HERE ALL ALONE!

I'LL LEAVE THIS HANDKERCHIEF. SHE CAN USE IT AS A TOWEL WHEN SHE COMES OUT OF THE WATER.

LEAVE TWO, SO SHE CAN HAVE A BLANKET.

WHAT IF THE ALLIGATORS TAKE HER BLANKET? IMPY SAID THERE WERE ALLIGATORS IN THE LAKE, AND THAT THEY WOULD EAT TIFFANY.

I NEVER SAID...

ALLIGATORS DON'T EAT SQUIRREL. BESIDES, WHAT WOULD **YOU** RATHER EAT—A STUFFED SQUIRREL, OR A TURKEY LEG?

BOO-HOO HOO!

•SNIFF•

IT WAS A TERRIBLE RIDE HOME. I KNEW I WAS IN TROUBLE, AND THAT I DESERVED IT.

WHEN WE GOT HOME, MOM AND DAD TOOK TURNS YELLING AT ME WHILE THE OTHER ONE TOOK CARE OF FELIX.

...CAN'T BELIEVE YOU'RE SO **SELFISH**...

...LIED TO US ABOUT SCHOOL, AND NOW **THIS**...

...YOUR BROTHER'S TOY **SQUIRREL**, OF ALL THINGS...

...MY OWN DAUGHTER WOULD BE SO **MEAN**...

I'M **SORRY**! I DIDN'T MEAN IT!

THAT WON'T CUT IT, NOT THIS TIME! AND IT'S NOT **ME** YOU SHOULD APOLOGIZE TO! GO TO YOUR BROTHER'S ROOM, AND **SEE** HOW DISTRAUGHT HE IS!

I DIDN'T HAVE TO GO TO HIS ROOM TO KNOW HOW HE FELT— OUR NEIGHBORS IN THE NEXT BUILDING PROBABLY KNEW.

FELIX, I'M SORRY. I'M REALLY SORRY.

GO TO YOUR ROOM, IMPY. JUST GO. YOU'VE DONE ENOUGH FOR TODAY.

FELIX CRIED ALL NIGHT LONG. I COULD HEAR MOM SOOTHING HIM, BUT HE COULDN'T CALM DOWN. I FELT WORSE THAN I EVER HAVE IN MY ENTIRE LIFE.

ALL ALONG, I THOUGHT I WAS THE KNIGHT IN THE STORY, DOING GOOD AND FIGHTING EVIL.

BUT REALLY, I WAS THE DRAGON. SPREADING MEANNESS AND EVIL ALL AROUND ME.

SUNDAY WAS A BLUR. FELIX AND THE PRINCESS SPENT THE WHOLE DAY AT THE LAKE LOOKING FOR TIFFANY. I TRIED TO HELP, BUT...

I DON'T WANT YOU HERE! GO AWAY!

EVERYONE STOPPED BY...KIT, CUSSIE, THE QUEEN...ANITA. NOBODY COULD FIND TIFFANY.

WHEN IT WAS TIME TO GO HOME, I SAW FELIX LEAVE HIS UNEATEN SANDWICH FROM LUNCH NEXT TO A TREE, AND I KNEW IT WAS FOR TIFFANY.

I HAD THE SINKING FEELING THAT SHE WAS GONE, GONE, GONE.

CHAPTER TEN

Sometimes a knight in shining armor has to re-assess their life goals. Maybe they can't handle this quest after all. Hey, it happens. What about being a hermit instead? Hermit sounds good.

IT WAS A RELIEF TO NOT HAVE TO GO TO SCHOOL FOR THREE DAYS.

THEN AGAIN...MAYBE IT WOULD BE WORSE TO STAY HOME.

SNIFF

C'MON, IMPY. YOU'RE COMING TO WORK WITH ME. GRAB YOUR HOMEWORK.

PENNY PINCHER
POOL · SPA

FLOOR COVER

NORMALLY, FELIX AND I LIKE GOING TO VISIT DAD AT WORK. WE LOUNGE AROUND IN THE EMPTY POOLS LIKE WE'RE RICH. AND I LIKE WATCHING DAD SCHMOOZING WITH THE CUSTOMERS.

TODAY, THOUGH, I JUST HID IN A HOT TUB LIKE A HERMIT IN A CAVE.

IT WAS PROBABLY BEST IF I JUST RETREATED FROM THE WORLD FOR A LITTLE WHILE. DON'T TALK TO ANYBODY. DON'T LOOK AT ANYBODY.

HERMIT CAVE

YES, THE HERMIT LIFE WOULD SUIT ME JUST FINE.

185

MY NEW ROUTINE WAS PRETTY SIMPLE. I WOKE UP, GOT DRESSED, AND ATE BREAKFAST.

I TRIED TO APOLOGIZE TO FELIX A FEW TIMES...

FELIX, I...

...BUT THAT DIDN'T GO OVER SO WELL.

I RODE TO WORK WITH DAD AND PRETENDED LIKE IT WAS TOTALLY NORMAL NOT TO TALK TO EACH OTHER AT ALL.

THEN I SETTLED INTO MY HOT TUB CAVE FOR THE DAY. AT LEAST THE HERMIT LIFE GAVE ME TIME TO CATCH UP ON MY HOMEWORK. MOM PACKED ME A LUNCH, SO I DIDN'T EVEN NEED TO LEAVE MY CAVE TO EAT.

WHEN WE GOT HOME, I WENT RIGHT TO MY ROOM. I DIDN'T EVEN COME OUT FOR DINNER. I'D RATHER BE HUNGRY THAN SIT AT THE DINNER TABLE WITH MY OWN FAMILY IGNORING ME.

I WASN'T ALLOWED TO WATCH TV OR USE THE INTERNET, BUT I DIDN'T CARE. HERMITS LIVED A BARREN EXISTENCE, SO I'D BETTER GET USED TO STARING AT WALLS.

BY THE THIRD DAY OF MY SUSPENSION, I WAS PRETTY USED TO THIS LIFE.

IMPY, YOU CAN SIT IN THE BREAK ROOM, YOU KNOW. YOU'LL BE MORE COMFORTABLE.

I LIKE THE HOT TUB.

I WAS JUST GETTING INTO A PARTICULARLY FASCINATING TIDBIT OF AMERICAN HISTORY WHEN...

DING

I NEED TO SPEAK TO THE MANAGER. SOME YAHOO SOLD ME THE WRONG PART FOR MY BROKEN SPA PUMP YESTERDAY.

I'M THE MANAGER ON DUTY.

OH, YEAH? WELL, I SPENT **FOUR HOURS** TRYING TO USE THE WRONG PART YESTERDAY.

MORON. WHO SPENDS FOUR HOURS TRYING TO USE THE WRONG PART?

LET'S TAKE A LOOK...WELL, SIR, ACCORDING TO YOUR OWNER'S MANUAL, THIS **SHOULD** BE THE RIGHT PART...

HEY. I JUST TOLD YOU, IT'S THE **WRONG PART**.

I DON'T KNOW **WHAT** KIND OF PEOPLE THEY GOT WORKING HERE NOWADAYS. AND YOU'RE A **MANAGER**? I DON'T KNOW WHERE YOU'RE FROM, BUT AROUND HERE, *AMIGO*...

HEY! YOU CAN'T TALK TO MY DAD THAT WAY! HE'S A **KNIGHT**! MAYBE **YOU** DON'T KNOW HOW TO FIX YOUR SPA! HUH? EVER THINK OF **THAT**?

IMPY! GET IN THE BREAK ROOM! **NOW**!

FINE!

SLAM!

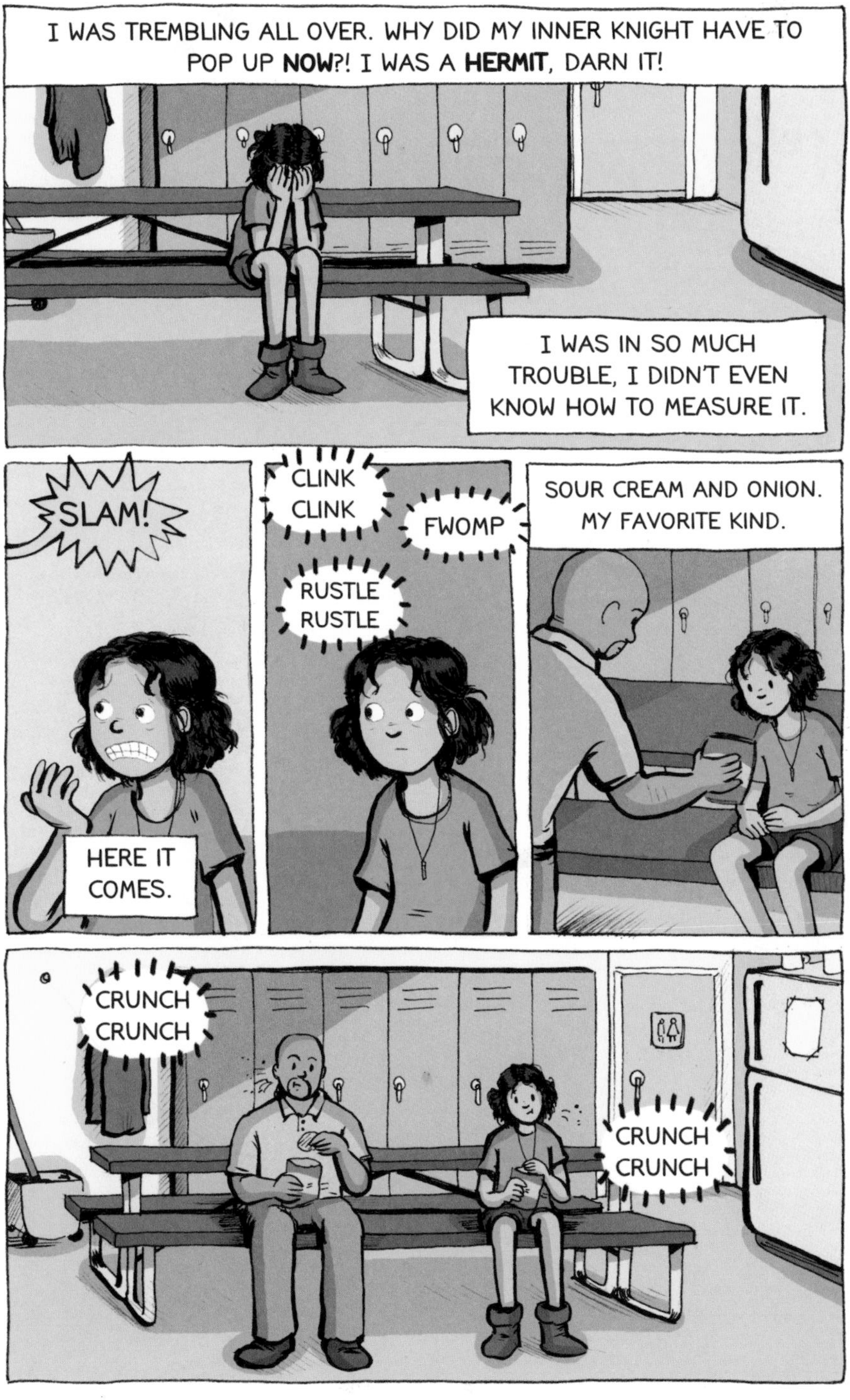
I WAS TREMBLING ALL OVER. WHY DID MY INNER KNIGHT HAVE TO POP UP **NOW**?! I WAS A **HERMIT**, DARN IT!
I WAS IN SO MUCH TROUBLE, I DIDN'T EVEN KNOW HOW TO MEASURE IT.
SLAM!
HERE IT COMES.
CLINK CLINK
FWOMP
RUSTLE RUSTLE
SOUR CREAM AND ONION. MY FAVORITE KIND.
CRUNCH CRUNCH
CRUNCH CRUNCH

CRUNCH
...

DAD?

HEH-HEH-HEH
HA-HA!

THE LOOK ON THAT GUY'S FACE! "MAYBE YOU DON'T KNOW HOW TO FIX YOUR SPA!" **HA-HA-HA!**

I THOUGHT I WAS GOING TO LAUGH TOO, BUT INSTEAD...

SOB

DADDY, I'M SORRY. I'M SO SORRY.

I DIDN'T MEAN ABOUT THE SPA GUY. BUT I DIDN'T HAVE TO TELL HIM THAT—HE KNEW.

OH, IMPY, YOU'RE A GOOD KID. YOU JUST... GOT LOST SOMEHOW.

I DON'T KNOW HOW TO GET **UN**-LOST. I DON'T KNOW WHAT TO DO.

IMPY...THERE'S A LOT OF ANGER AND HATRED IN THE WORLD. YOU KNOW THAT BY NOW.

BUT WE ARE KNIGHTS. IT'S **OUR** JOB TO MAKE THE WORLD BETTER. YOU'LL FIGURE OUT A WAY TO FIX THE MISTAKES YOU'VE MADE.

BUT **HOW**?

CHIVALRY. HONESTY. BRAVERY. RIGHT?

BIG HELP, DAD.

AND YET, I FELT A LITTLE BETTER.

WE STILL DIDN'T TALK ON THE CAR RIDE HOME, BUT THE SILENCE FELT A LITTLE DIFFERENT NOW. NICER.

I WENT TO MY ROOM WHEN WE GOT HOME. I WORKED UP SOME COURAGE, AND WHEN I HEARD EVERYONE SITTING DOWN TO DINNER...

191

MY VOICE SOUNDED CREAKY, LIKE I HADN'T USED IT IN DAYS.

MOM? DAD? YOU KNOW HOW YOU SAID I COULD GO BACK TO HOMESCHOOLING WHENEVER I WANT? WELL...I WANT TO. I DON'T WANT TO GO BACK TO SCHOOL.

NO.

NO?

YOU MADE A MISTAKE, IMOGENE—LOTS OF MISTAKES—AND NOW YOU HAVE TO FACE THE MUSIC. YOU CAN'T JUST RUN AND HIDE FROM YOUR PROBLEMS.

RUNNING AND HIDING WAS BASICALLY MY NEW LIFE PLAN, SO THIS WAS UNWELCOME NEWS.

BUT I COULD STAY HOME AND HELP YOU AND DAD, LIKE BEFORE.

HELLLLLLOOOOOOOO! WE DON'T WANT YOU HERE!

FELIX...

BUT...

THAT'S MY FINAL ANSWER, IMPY. **YOU** MADE THE DECISION TO GO TO SCHOOL. **YOU** MADE THE DECISION TO MAKE MEAN DRAWINGS OF YOUR FRIENDS, **YOU** MADE THE DECISION TO BE CRUEL TO YOUR BROTHER. YOUR ACTIONS HAVE CONSEQUENCES, AND YOU HAVE TO FACE THEM.

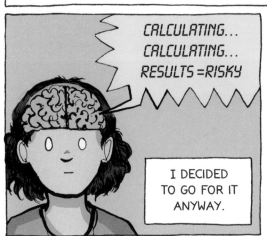

CALCULATING...
CALCULATING...
RESULTS = RISKY

I DECIDED TO GO FOR IT ANYWAY.

DAD?

HEY! DON'T YOU **DARE** ASK YOUR FATHER, WHEN I JUST GAVE YOU AN ANSWER! THE ANSWER IS **NO!**

IT'S WHAT I EXPECTED. I FIGURED THERE WAS NO AVOIDING IT. IT WAS WORTH A SHOT, ANYWAY.

MAYBE I COULDN'T RUN, BUT I COULD HIDE. I DECIDED TO USE HERMIT MODE AT SCHOOL TOO. BASICALLY, HERMIT MODE INVOLVES NOT TALKING TO ANYBODY AND IGNORING DIRTY LOOKS.

IGNORING WHISPERS IN THE HALL.

POOR!

IGNORING CERTAIN COMMENTS FROM CERTAIN TEACHERS.

I SEE OUR RESIDENT ARTIST IS BACK IN CLASS. NEXT TIME, PLEASE DRAW ME FROM THE LEFT—THAT'S MY GOOD SIDE.

IGNORING NOTES FROM KINDA-SORTA FORMER LOVE INTERESTS.

I don't have a good side!

IGNORING FORMER KINDA-SORTA FRIENDS.

IMOGENE...

THAT WAS MEAN OF HER TO STEAL YOUR NOTEBOOK AND PUT THOSE DRAWINGS UP. I JUST WANTED YOU TO KNOW, I DIDN'T DO IT.

IGNORING ANYTHING THAT MADE ME FEEL BAD.

GOOD, BAD, INDIFFERENT—MY GOAL WAS TO IGNORE IT ALL AND BECOME INVISIBLE. I'D LIVE OUT THE REST OF SIXTH GRADE THIS WAY, AND MAYBE MOM WOULD LET ME STAY HOME FOR SEVENTH. IF SHE WASN'T STILL MAD AT ME BY THEN, THAT IS.

I USED HERMIT MODE AT FAIRE TOO. ON DAYS THAT WE WENT THERE AFTER SCHOOL TO SET UP, I DIDN'T TRY TO TALK TO CUSSIE OR SWORD FIGHT WITH DAD OR KIT. I SAT IN THE BACK OF THE SHOPPE AND DID MY HOMEWORK.

ONE PERSON I **COULDN'T** IGNORE...

IMOGENE, VIOLET IS HERE FOR YOUR TUTORING SESSION.

PART OF MY PUNISHMENT, BESIDES NOT BEING A SQUIRE, NO TV, AND NO INTERNET WAS TUTORING IN SCIENCE. FROM THE PRINCESS HERSELF.

SO YOU HAVE TO GIVE A PRESENTATION ON COPERNICUS, HUH? I BORROWED THESE BOOKS FROM CUSSIE.

THANKS.

FEWEST WORDS POSSIBLE WITHOUT GETTING IN TROUBLE FOR BEING RUDE.

THAT'S HOW LIFE WENT ON FOR A WHILE. IT WASN'T SO BAD BEING INVISIBLE, IF YOU LIKE THAT ZEN, QUIET KIND OF LIFE.

EVENTUALLY I REACHED FULL INVISIBILITY LEVELS AT SCHOOL.

POOR!

...**ALMOST** FULL INVISIBILITY.

I STARTED DOING BETTER IN MY CLASSES. EVEN SCIENCE, BELIEVE IT OR NOT.

B+

THE WORST PARTS WERE AT NIGHT AFTER I FINISHED MY HOMEWORK.

I WAS BACK TO EATING DINNER AT THE TABLE. EVERYONE TALKED TO ME NOW...

FELIX? WOULD YOU LIKE SOME MASHED POTATOES?

WELL, **EXCEPT** FELIX.

BUT CONVERSATIONS WERE **WEIRD**, AND EVERYTHING FELT DIFFERENT.

IMOGENE, PLEASE PASS THE SALT.

MOM: ODDLY FORMAL

DAD: SAD SMILE

FELIX: OUTRIGHT HOSTILITY

ME: FEEL LIKE AN OUTSIDER

THE WORST PART WAS, I DIDN'T KNOW HOW LONG THIS WOULD GO ON. I WAS ALREADY BEING PUNISHED—HOW LONG WOULD THEY STAY MAD AT ME? FOREVER?

MAYBE THEY'D NEVER SEE ME THE SAME WAY AGAIN.

IN MY ROOM, WITH ALL MY HOMEWORK DONE...

NO STARS AGAIN. STUPID DR. MACGREGOR.

...I MOSTLY WROTE IN MY JOURNAL. AND SOMETIMES DREW. I DREW A LOT OF PICTURES OF TIFFANY, I GUESS BECAUSE I FELT GUILTY.

ALL-IN ALL, NOT BAD, THE HERMIT LIFE.

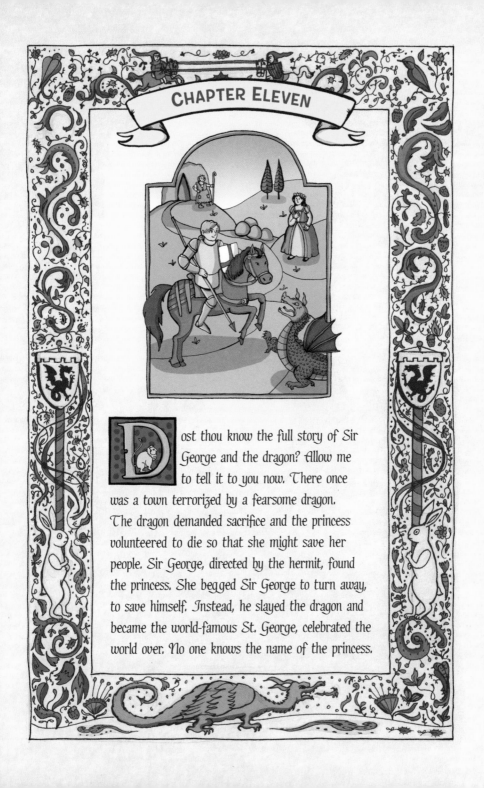

CHAPTER ELEVEN

Dost thou know the full story of Sir George and the dragon? Allow me to tell it to you now. There once was a town terrorized by a fearsome dragon. The dragon demanded sacrifice and the princess volunteered to die so that she might save her people. Sir George, directed by the hermit, found the princess. She begged Sir George to turn away, to save himself. Instead, he slayed the dragon and became the world-famous St. George, celebrated the world over. No one knows the name of the princess.

I KNOW I BASICALLY ONLY SCOOPED UP HORSE POOP, BUT I MISSED MY SQUIRE DUTIES AT FAIRE. I MISSED THE K.I.T. KIDS. I MISSED ANITA.

THERE WERE ONLY A FEW WEEKS LEFT OF FAIRE, BUT I WAS AFRAID TO ASK MOM AND DAD ABOUT GOING BACK TO BEING A SQUIRE.

WE JUST CAN'T **TRUST** YOU, IMOGENE.

YOU'RE NOT READY TO BE A SQUIRE.

SO I DIDN'T ASK. I JUST STAYED INVISIBLE.

WHEN I COULDN'T STAND HIDING IN THE SHOPPE ANY LONGER, I WENT TO THE ONE PLACE WHERE A HERMIT COULD BE AT PEACE AT A RENAISSANCE FAIRE.

HERMIT CAVE

PRIVIES

HEY, MOPEY! YOU'VE BEEN HANGING AROUND MY CAVE FOR TWENTY MINUTES NOW! WHAT ARE YOU, MY HERMIT APPRENTICE?

SOUNDS GOOD TO ME.

WELL, FORGET IT. HERMITS WORK ALONE. CHECK THE JOB DESCRIPTION.

FINE.

IMPY, IMPY, IMPY. COME HERE. I KNOW IT'S BEEN A TOUGH FEW WEEKS FOR YOU. TALK TO ME.

SCOOCH

I GUESS I WASN'T A GOOD HERMIT, BECAUSE THAT'S ALL IT TOOK FOR ME TO START TALKING.

IT'S JUST...I THOUGHT I WAS THE KNIGHT BUT THEN IT TURNS OUT I'M THE DRAGON SO NOW I'M BEING THE HERMIT SO I DON'T HAVE TO TALK TO ANYONE EVER AGAIN.

COME AGAIN?

I THINK...

I THINK I'M NOT A NICE PERSON.

IMOGENE. YOU ARE **NOT** A BAD PERSON. WE ALL HAVE A LITTLE DRAGON INSIDE OF US. IT'S JUST A MATTER OF KEEPING IT TAMED.

WHAT IF IT'S A LARGER DRAGON THAN USUAL? WHAT IF I'M, LIKE, 90% DRAGON?

YOU'RE TRAINING TO BE A KNIGHT, AREN'T YOU? SLAY THAT SON OF A...

...GUN!

I'M NOT A VERY GOOD KNIGHT-IN-TRAINING.

NUDGE

YOU'RE NOT A VERY GOOD HERMIT, EITHER.

YOU KNOW, YOU'VE TALKED ABOUT THE DRAGON, THE KNIGHT, AND THE HERMIT. THERE'S ONE CHARACTER IN THE STORY YOU **HAVEN'T** MENTIONED.

UM...**NO**. IN CASE YOU HAVEN'T NOTICED, I DON'T **DO** PRINCESS.

OH?

IN THE STORY, THE PRINCESS NEVER **DOES** ANYTHING. SHE GIVES UP—SHE DOESN'T TRY TO FIGHT THE DRAGON OR ANYTHING. SHE'S STUPID.

ON THE CONTRARY, **I** THINK SHE'S THE BRAVEST CHARACTER IN THE STORY.

HA-HA.

'TIS TRUE! THE PRINCESS **VOLUNTEERS TO GET EATEN BY A DRAGON!** SHE WALKS BRAVELY INTO THE VERY MOUTH OF DANGER WITH NARY A THOUGHT FOR HERSELF. SHE'S NOT LOOKING FOR FAME, OR TO BE A HERO—SHE'S JUST A NICE PERSON TRYING TO SAVE HER VILLAGE. **KINDNESS** IS THE TRUEST FORM OF BRAVERY.

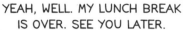
YEAH, WELL. MY LUNCH BREAK IS OVER. SEE YOU LATER.

I SAT IN THE BACK OF THE SHOPPE AND DOODLED IN MY JOURNAL THE REST OF THE DAY.

GOOD DAY, LADY IMOGENE!

SERIOUSLY, **WHY** IS SHE SO NICE?

I DON'T DESERVE IT. NOT AFTER EVERYTHING I'VE DONE.

FELIX SPENDS ALL HIS TIME PLAYING HIS VIDEO GAME NOW. IT'S LIKE HE'S GONE INTO HIS OWN HERMIT MODE.

I WISH I COULD TAKE IT ALL BACK.

I KNEW I COULDN'T, BUT...

...MAYBE I COULD MAKE HIM FEEL BETTER.

To Felix
I'm sorry.

Love,
Impy

FELIX, I MADE SOMETHING FOR YOU.

RIP

RIP

SEE? I KNEW KINDNESS WAS A WASTE OF TIME.

I'D JUST GO BACK TO BEING INVISIBLE.

THE HARDEST TIME TO BE INVISIBLE AT SCHOOL IS AT LUNCH. LOTS OF KIDS IN ONE ROOM + MINIMAL ADULT SUPERVISION = **A VERY BAD IDEA**.

USUALLY I ASK THE TEACHER ON DUTY IF I CAN USE THE BATHROOM, AND THEN I TAKE MY SWEET OLD TIME COMING BACK.

BUT EVEN THE BRAVEST OF KNIGHTS CAN'T LAST TOO LONG IN A SCHOOL BATHROOM...

UGH! WHAT'S THAT **SMELL**?

...SO THAT USUALLY LEAVES ME WITH SOME TIME TO KILL. TODAY I TOOK A DIFFERENT ROUTE BACK TO THE CAFETERIA TO TAKE UP A FEW MINUTES.

AGHHHHH!

MS. VEGA, THIS IS A MEETING OF THE SCIENCE OLYMPIAD. AS YOU ARE NOT A MEMBER OF THE SCIENCE OLYMPIAD, PLEASE RETURN TO THE CAFETERIA OR YOU'LL RECEIVE A DETENTION.

OH... OK.

ANITA HAS... **FRIENDS**. I DIDN'T RUIN HER LIFE, I GUESS.

THERE'S ABOUT TEN MINUTES BETWEEN THE END OF LUNCH AND THE NEXT PERIOD, SO ALL THE SIXTH GRADERS HAVE TO WAIT AROUND IN THE COURTYARD. IT LOOKED LIKE LUNCH WAS JUST LETTING OUT, SO I SAT DOWN, FELLING A LITTLE STUNNED.

NO, DON'T. LEAVE HER ALONE— SHE'S JUST SITTING THERE.

HEY IMOGENE! THINK FAST!

PFFFFFT!

HA!

HA!

THE COURTYARD GOT VERY QUIET. I GOT TO MY FEET.

THE QUESTION WAS, WHAT DO I DO **NOW**?

QUIET! YOU'RE ALL DRIVING ME CRAZY!! LET ME **THINK**!

SOMETIMES, WHEN YOU DON'T KNOW WHAT TO DO...

...AVOIDANCE IS THE ONLY WAY TO GO.

OH MY GOD, WHAT A **FREAK**!

JUST FOR THAT, I THREW THE APPLE CHUNKS A LITTLE HIGHER.

WHAT THE HECK, WHY NOT.

SASHA, THROW ME THAT APPLE IN YOUR HAND.

SURE, I'D NEVER SUCCESSFULLY JUGGLED FOUR ITEMS BEFORE. BUT WHAT DID I HAVE TO LOSE?

DON'T DO IT, SASHA.

C'MON, SASHA! A NICE GENTLE TOSS.

TOSS

YAHOO!

RRRIIIIIINNNNGGG!

YAY!

YAY!

HEY. CAN YOU TEACH ME HOW TO DO THAT?

THAT'S SO COOL!

WHATEVER. YOU'RE STILL A LOSER.

PSSSST PSSSST PSSST

CRUUUUUNCH!

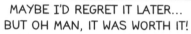

MAYBE I'D REGRET IT LATER... BUT OH MAN, IT WAS WORTH IT!

TODAY WAS A FAIRE DAY AFTER SCHOOL, WHICH MEANT— ANOTHER TUTORING SESSION. BUT EVEN THE PRINCESS COULDN'T KILL MY GOOD MOOD.

HERE'S THE PAPER FOR MY COPERNICUS PRESENTATION, IF YOU WANT TO READ IT.

YOU'RE PEPPY TODAY!

GOOD DAY AT SCHOOL?

IT WAS OK.

I THINK YOUR PAPER LOOKS GOOD! ARE YOU READY FOR THE PRESENTATION?

I GUESS SO. NOT LIKE IT MATTERS ANYWAY. THE TEACHER **HATES** ME.

WELL, IT'S NOT HIS JOB TO **LIKE** YOU. AND IT'S NOT YOUR JOB TO LIKE **HIM**. NOT EVERYONE IN LIFE IS GOING TO LIKE YOU, YOU KNOW.

OH. I'VE LEARNED **THAT** LESSON ALREADY, THANKS.

I WAS GOING TO WAIT UNTIL LATER TO GIVE THIS TO YOU, BUT... HERE. IT'S A PRESENT FOR ACING YOUR TEST LAST WEEK.

I GOT A B+.

JUST OPEN IT.

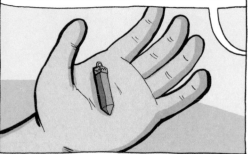

I KNOW YOU HAVE A CRYSTAL FOR LUCK. THIS ONE'S AN AMETHYST TO BRING YOU JOY. LUCK AND JOY WILL GET YOU THROUGH A LOT OF THINGS IN LIFE.

THAT'S REALLY NICE OF YOU...BUT I CAN'T KEEP IT.

DON'T BE SILLY! OF COURSE YOU CAN!

NO! IT'S...FIRST THE JOURNAL, NOW THIS. I KNOW YOU'RE NOT RICH—YOU LIVE IN A TRAILER WITH KIT. SO HOW COME YOU KEEP BUYING ME STUFF WHEN YOU BARELY KNOW ME?

"WHEN I'M A TOTAL JERK TO YOU," I DIDN'T ADD.

I LEARNED A LONG TIME AGO THAT MONEY DOESN'T MAKE YOU HAPPY. HERE, LET'S PUT IT ON.

HOW COME YOU'RE SO NICE TO ME ALL THE TIME? TO **EVERYONE** ALL THE TIME? DON'T YOU GET **TIRED** OF BEING NICE?

FOR THE FIRST TIME, I SAW HER SMILE SLIP A LITTLE.

HMMPH.

I DIDN'T...I WASN'T...I DIDN'T HAVE THE BEST FAMILY GROWING UP. YOU'RE VERY LUCKY TO HAVE THE FAMILY YOU DO.

I'M SERIOUS! LOTS OF PEOPLE AREN'T AS LUCKY AS YOU ARE.

SO, I WAS IN A BAD PLACE WHEN I WAS A TEENAGER...

AND THEN ONE DAY I CAME HERE! WELL, NOT **HERE** HERE—TO THE RENAISSANCE FAIRE.

AND IT WAS LIKE COMING HOME. I FOUND MY PEOPLE, AND I FOUND HAPPINESS. I LEFT MY STEPFATHER'S HOUSE AND NEVER LOOKED BACK.

A FEW YEARS LATER I MET KIT—AND HE TOLD ME ALL ABOUT **YOU**.

THAT'S WHY I TRY TO BE HAPPY, AND THAT'S WHY I BUY YOU PRESENTS. I CAN CHOOSE MY OWN FAMILY NOW. I WON'T LET MY STEPFATHER TAKE MY HAPPINESS AWAY FROM ME. I **CHOOSE** TO BE HAPPY.

I COULD TELL YOUR FAMILY WAS IMPORTANT TO HIM...SO, YOU ARE IMPORTANT TO **ME**.

CHAPTER TWELVE

Sometimes in the midst of a dark thicket, a knight-in-training may try—just TRY—being a princess for a spell. Even if this knight-in-training never, ever, EVER thought of themselves as a princess type. Ever. Not ever... but just maybe, it might lead the hero toward the path out of darkness.

IT'S HARDER TO CHOOSE HAPPINESS AT MIDDLE SCHOOL THAN AT FAIRE. BUT WHAT DID I HAVE TO LOSE? IT'S NOT LIKE I HAD ANY FRIENDS ANYWAY. BESIDES, I THINK I HAD WORKED THROUGH ALL THE STAGES OF MY SOCIAL DISGRACE.

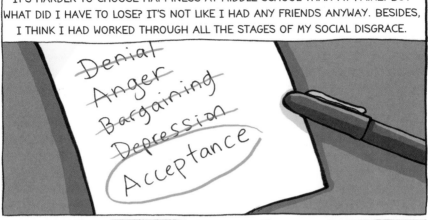

I DECIDED TO PRETEND I WAS DOING STREET AND PLAYING A CHARACTER, AND JUST STARTED CHATTING TO ANYBODY AND EVERYBODY, INCLUDING:

RANDOM STRANGERS,

MATHLETES,

JOCKS,

NICE DAY, ISN'T IT!

I HEARD YOU WON LAST NIGHT—WELL DONE!

GOOD LUCK AT SOCCER TRYOUTS!

FORMER ALMOST-FRIENDS

FORMER ALMOST-LOVE INTERESTS

EVEN DRAGONS.

BLINK

I THOUGHT YOU MIGHT LIKE THE NEWEST ANIMAL ANTICS BOOK.

HEY, PICASSO.

THAT WAS A GOOD LESSON TODAY, DR. M. I LEARNED A LOT.

AND EVEN BIGGER, MORE FEROCIOUS DRAGONS.

NICE JOB IN THE MOCK TRIAL TODAY.

DON'T TALK TO ME, **LOSER**! IF YOU'RE TRYING TO BE POPULAR BY PRETENDING TO BE **NICE**, FORGET IT.

PSSSST PSSST

THANK YOU VERY MUCH! HAVE A NICE DAY!

MY NICENESS SEEMED TO HAVE EXACTLY ZERO EFFECT ON **ANYBODY**...BUT ESPECIALLY THE TWO PEOPLE I'D **ACTUALLY** REALLY HURT.

ANITA TURNED OUT TO BE THE SILENT TYPE.

ANITA, I'M **SORRY**.

I MADE YOU THIS WREATH...

I'LL TAKE ONE COOKIE, PLEASE. KEEP THE CHANGE.

Science Olympiad Bake Sale!

HEY, THIS IS A $10 BILL!

FELIX, ON THE OTHER HAND, WAS MORE OF THE "THROWING" TYPE.

FELIX, I GOT YOU A COOKIE...

I PICKED YOU UP A BOOK AT THE LIBRARY...

AAAAAGH!

AAAAAGH!

DO YOU WANT TO SWORD FIGH....

UM, NEVER MIND.

I HAD ONE LAST IDEA ON HOW TO MAKE THINGS UP TO FELIX.

MOM? I KNOW I'M STILL GROUNDED, BUT...COULD I USE THE INTERNET?

IS IT FOR SCHOOL?

NOT EXACTLY. BUT IT'S IMPORTANT.

PLEASE?

SCOOCH

WOW—**THAT'S** WHAT TIFFANY USED TO LOOK LIKE?

AS I GOT READY FOR BED THAT NIGHT—NO STARS AGAIN, SURPRISE—

I RACKED MY BRAIN FOR IDEAS ON HOW TO MAKE THINGS UP WITH ANITA. BUT I HAD NOTHING. MAYBE OUR FRIENDSHIP WAS A LOST CAUSE.

BEFORE I KNEW IT, IT WAS THE LAST WEEK OF FAIRE. THE END OF FAIRE IS ALWAYS SAD. IT'S LIKE THE DAY AFTER CHRISTMAS, EXCEPT ALL YOUR TOYS GET TAKEN AWAY FROM YOU.

NOT HELPING MY MOOD ANY...

SO MY MOM WILL DRIVE US ALL ON SATURDAY MORNING. FIRST WE'LL WALK AROUND, AND THEN WE'LL WATCH SOME SHOWS.

AND ANY **UNINVITED LOSERS** BETTER STAY AWAY FROM MY PARTY.

SHE HAD NOTHING TO FEAR. I PLANNED ON STAYING **FAR, FAR** AWAY FROM THEM AT FAIRE.

AHEM

THIS IS A SCIENCE CLASS, NOT A MALL FOOD COURT. WE WILL NOW HEAR OUR TWO REPORTS ON GALILEO AND COPERNICUS. MR. KUO, YOU'RE UP FIRST.

GALILEO GALILEI WAS BORN IN 1564 IN PISA, ITALY. HE DIED IN 1642...

GALILEO WENT TO JAIL FOR SAYING THE EARTH REVOLVED AROUND THE SUN. HE...

ODDLY ENOUGH, I WASN'T THAT NERVOUS ABOUT GIVING MY SPEECH. A FEW WEEKS AGO, I WOULD HAVE BEEN TERRIFIED, BUT NOW I DIDN'T CARE SO MUCH. ONE OF THE BENEFITS OF GIVING UP ON MAKING FRIENDS, I GUESS.

CLAP
CLAP
CLAP

THANK YOU, MR. KUO. MS. VEGA, YOU'RE UP.

...OK, SO I WAS A **LITTLE** NERVOUS. I KEPT MY EYES ON MY PAPER.

NICOLAUS COPERNICUS WAS BORN IN 1473 IN POLAND.

HE IS BEST KNOWN FOR BEING THE FIRST SCIENTIST TO SAY THAT THE SUN WAS THE CENTER OF THE UNIVERSE, NOT THE EARTH. THIS WAS BIG NEWS BACK THEN.

HERE'S A PICTURE OF HIS MAP OF THE UNIVERSE.

THE REST OF MY SPEECH WAS KIND OF A BLUR, BUT I GOT THROUGH IT ALL.

CLAP
CLAP
CLAP

THANK YOU, MS. VEGA. YOU MAY SIT DOWN.

FINAL QUESTION FOR YOU BOTH: WHY DO YOU THINK I ASSIGNED YOU THESE SCIENTISTS IN PARTICULAR? MR. KUO?

UM...BECAUSE WE'RE STUDYING THE PLANETS?

NO. MS. VEGA?

BECAUSE...

EVEN THOUGH WE'RE JUST KIDS, WE CAN BE GOOD SCIENTISTS, LIKE ANITA?

EYEROLL

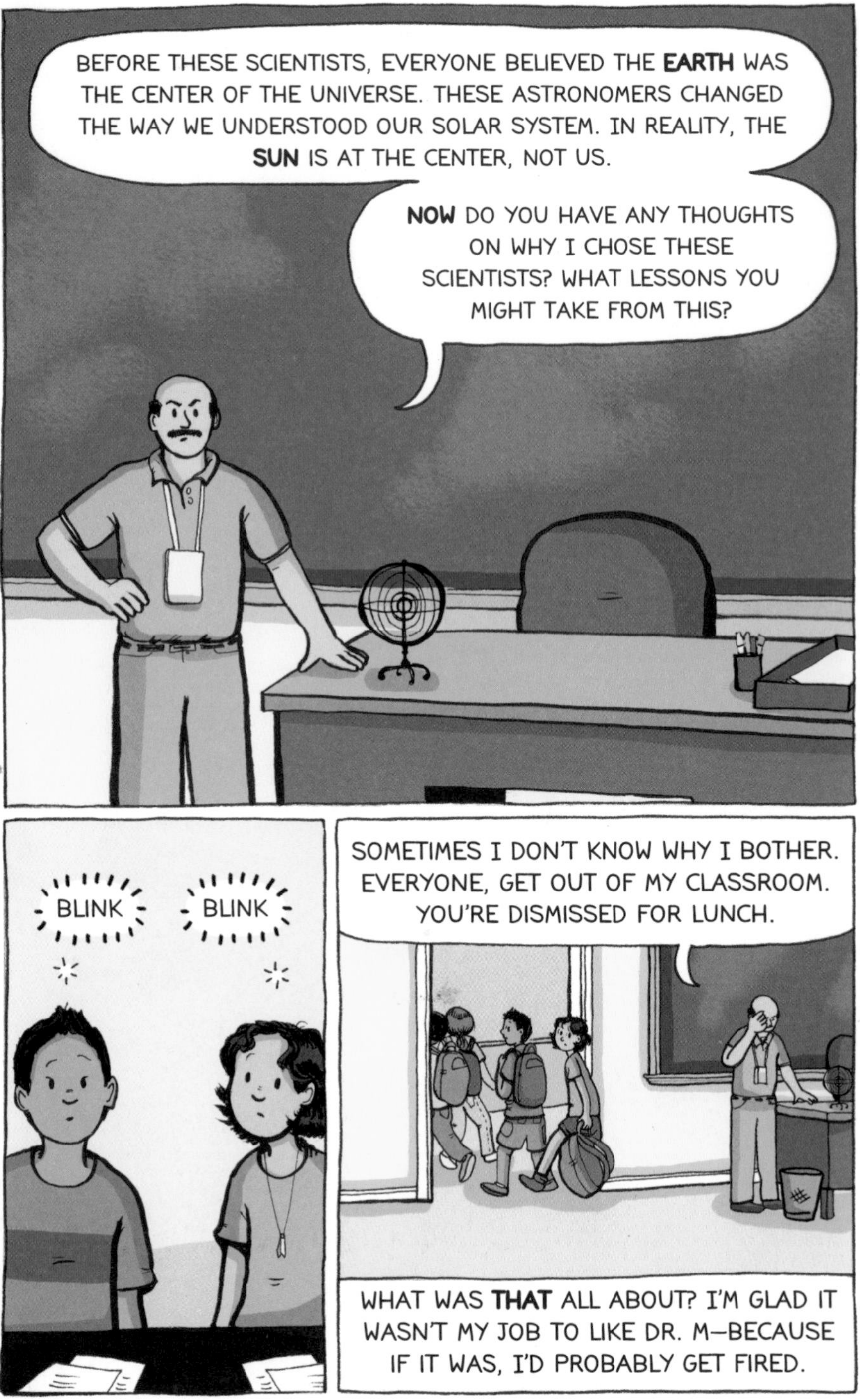
BEFORE THESE SCIENTISTS, EVERYONE BELIEVED THE **EARTH** WAS THE CENTER OF THE UNIVERSE. THESE ASTRONOMERS CHANGED THE WAY WE UNDERSTOOD OUR SOLAR SYSTEM. IN REALITY, THE **SUN** IS AT THE CENTER, NOT US.
NOW DO YOU HAVE ANY THOUGHTS ON WHY I CHOSE THESE SCIENTISTS? WHAT LESSONS YOU MIGHT TAKE FROM THIS?
BLINK
BLINK
SOMETIMES I DON'T KNOW WHY I BOTHER. EVERYONE, GET OUT OF MY CLASSROOM. YOU'RE DISMISSED FOR LUNCH.
WHAT WAS **THAT** ALL ABOUT? I'M GLAD IT WASN'T MY JOB TO LIKE DR. M—BECAUSE IF IT WAS, I'D PROBABLY GET FIRED.

EVEN THOUGH IT WAS THE LAST WEEK OF FAIRE, WE STILL WENT TO THE SHOPPE SOMETIMES AFTER SCHOOL. WE JUST DID MORE PACKING UP THAN RESTOCKING.

IMPY, THIS CAME TO THE APARTMENT TODAY FOR YOU.

WHY DON'T YOU GO GIVE IT TO HIM?

FELIX? I GOT SOMETHING FOR YOU. I KNOW IT'S NOT THE SAME, BUT I THOUGHT MAYBE...

223

IT WAS A NICE GESTURE, IMPY. JUST GIVE HIM SOME TIME.

I **HAVE** GIVEN HIM TIME. HE'S **NEVER** GOING TO FORGIVE ME.

OF COURSE HE'LL FORGIVE YOU. HE **WANTS** TO FORGIVE YOU. YOU'RE HIS HERO, YOU KNOW.

HMMPH.

WHY DON'T YOU TRY TALKING TO HIM AGAIN?

I'VE TRIED TALKING TO HIM A **MILLION TIMES**!

MAKE IT A MILLION AND ONE.

•SIGH•

FELIX?

·SNIFF·

I DID SOMETHING STUPID. I'M SORRY. I WASN'T THINKING. PLEASE FORGIVE ME.

CAN I WATCH YOU PLAY?

SCOOCH

HOW DO YOU MAKE THE FIREBALLS COME OUT?

SNIFF

YOU JUST PRESS A4, AND THEN THE ARROW BUTTON.

CHAPTER THIRTEEN

Dearest fellow travelers, it saddens me to say we are nearing the end of our journey together. If thou believest in happily ever afters...you obviously have never attended Middle School, but perhaps our hero will come close enough.

THE FINAL WEEKEND OF FAIRE. I COULDN'T BELIEVE IT WAS OVER ALREADY.

IMOGENE, COME AND HAVE A SEAT. WE WANT TO TALK TO YOU.

UH-OH.

YOU'VE MADE SOME MISTAKES OVER THE PAST FEW WEEKS—SOME BIG ONES. BUT YOUR GRADES ARE GETTING BETTER, AND WE'VE SEEN HOW YOU'RE TRYING WITH FELIX.

SO—WE'RE REINSTATING YOUR SQUIRE DUTIES.

REALLY?

REALLY. HERE'S YOUR COSTUME BACK. WE TRUST THAT YOU'LL DO US PROUD.

I WAS GLAD I GOT TO BE A SQUIRE AGAIN FOR THE LAST WEEKEND... BUT I COULDN'T HELP FEELING LIKE I DIDN'T DESERVE IT SOMEHOW.

IF PERHAPS YOU'RE THINKING THAT I FORGOT ABOUT MIKA'S BIRTHDAY PARTY TODAY—YOU'D BE **WRONG**. BUT I FIGURED I COULD HIDE OUT AT THE K.I.T. SCHOOL IN CASE...

OH. FIE!

...I HAPPENED TO SEE THEM.

GOOD DAY, IMOGENE! I SEE YOU'RE A SQUIRE ONCE AGAIN. HUZZAH! DOES THIS MEAN YOUR PRESENTATION ON COPERNICUS WAS A SUCCESS?

OH, HEH-HEH. GOOD DAY! I **THINK** SO...THANKS FOR YOUR HELP, VIOLET. FOR EVERYTHING.

IT WAS MY PLEASURE. YOU **SHOULD** THANK CUSSIE FOR THE BOOKS.

OH YEAH. HOW COME YOU HAD THOSE BOOKS, ANYWAY, CUSSIE?

WELL, I **AM** SOMETHING OF AN EXPERT ON THE MAN. HOW DO YOU THINK I GOT MY NAME?

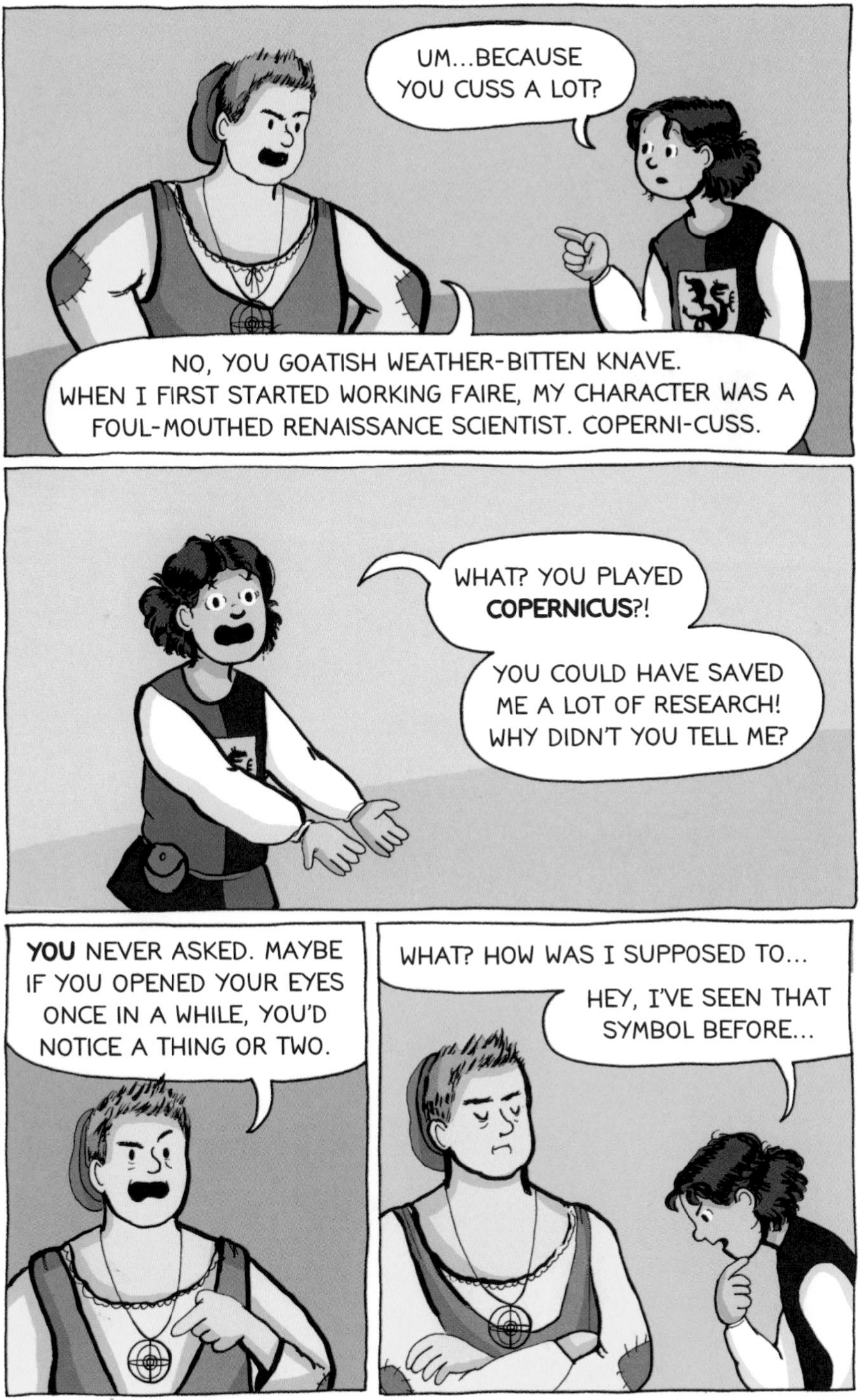
UM...BECAUSE YOU CUSS A LOT?
NO, YOU GOATISH WEATHER-BITTEN KNAVE. WHEN I FIRST STARTED WORKING FAIRE, MY CHARACTER WAS A FOUL-MOUTHED RENAISSANCE SCIENTIST. COPERNI-CUSS.
WHAT? YOU PLAYED **COPERNICUS**?!
YOU COULD HAVE SAVED ME A LOT OF RESEARCH! WHY DIDN'T YOU TELL ME?
YOU NEVER ASKED. MAYBE IF YOU OPENED YOUR EYES ONCE IN A WHILE, YOU'D NOTICE A THING OR TWO.
WHAT? HOW WAS I SUPPOSED TO...
HEY, I'VE SEEN THAT SYMBOL BEFORE...

THAT'S FROM COPERNICUS! I USED THAT IN MY PAPER!

I KNOW IT'S HARD TO GET THROUGH THAT KNUCKLEBRAINED TEENAGE HEAD OF YOURS...

TEENAGE!

...BUT IF YOU OPEN YOUR EYES TO THE WORLD AROUND YOU, YOU'LL NOTICE A LOT OF THINGS. THAT'S WHY I WEAR THIS SYMBOL, TO REMIND MYSELF OF THE REVOLUTIONARY CONCEPT OF THE HELIOCENTRIC MODEL.

MEANING...

MEANING, YOU'RE NOT THE CENTER OF THE DAMN UNIVERSE!

OH.

OOHHHHH!

FINALLY IT SINKS IN!

THAT'S WHY THE DOCTOR MADE US DO THOSE REPORTS! HE WAS TRYING TO SAY WE WERE BEING SELF-CENTERED, IN A WAY THAT WOULDN'T GET HIM FIRED.

JERK.

I **HAD** BEEN THINKING ABOUT MYSELF A LOT RECENTLY...HOW **I** WAS FEELING AT SCHOOL, HOW **I** WANTED TO AVOID MIKA AND HER POSSE TODAY...

WHEN MAYBE I SHOULD HAVE BEEN THINKING ABOUT SOMEBODY ELSE.

UH-OH. I GOTTA GO!

OI! ARE YOU GOING TO LEAVE ALL THESE CHILDREN HERE? WE HAVE TO GO TO THE ROYAL COURT! REMEMBER, YOU'RE NOT THE CENTER OF THE DAMN UNIVERSE!

OH. RIGHT. UH, DRAGON HUNT, EVERYBODY! LET'S GO ON A DRAGON HUNT!

IT SEEMED LIKE IT TOOK **FOREVER** FOR THOSE KIDS TO GET ORGANIZED. SHOES HAD TO BE TIED, SWORDS FOUND. ONE KID REFUSED TO MOVE WITHOUT A PIGGYBACK RIDE.

WHAT DO HIS PARENTS **FEED** THIS KID? ROCKS?

I HAD TO WARN ANITA BEFORE...

TOO LATE.

ISN'T IT ENOUGH YOU BOTHER ME AT SCHOOL? DO YOU HAVE TO HARASS ME IN MY OWN PRIVATE TIME, TOO?

LOOKS LIKE ANITA'S LETTING HER KNIGHT OUT TOO! MAYBE SHE DOESN'T NEED MY HELP...MAYBE I CAN JUST STAY HIDDEN...

THEN I OPENED MY EYES AND LOOKED A LITTLE CLOSER.

ALMOST CRYING

LIP TREMBLING

SHAKING A LITTLE

NAY. EVERYONE CAN USE A LITTLE BACKUP.

COME, KNIGHTS-IN-TRAINING...

CHARGE!

THOU VILLAINOUS EARTH-VEXING PIGEON EGG! ART THOU HARASSING LADY ANITA, ONE OF THE KINGDOM'S MOST HONORED CITIZENS?

IMOGENE! LEAVE IT ALONE!

OH MY GOD.

NAY! I SHALL NOT LEAVE IT ALONE! DOST THOU NOT KNOW THAT LADY ANITA IS BOTH A PERSONAGE OF GREAT NOBILITY, **AND** A FORMIDABLE SWORDSWOMAN?

IN FACT, I SHALL **PROVE** HER POWER TO YOU!

WHAT IS GOING ON RIGHT NOW?

I, IMOGENE, SQUIRE TO SIR HUGO, KNIGHT OF HER MAJESTY'S REALM, DO CHALLENGE YOU, LADY ANITA, TO A DUEL!

I DECLINE.

WOULDST THOU DENY THESE CITIZENS THE PRIVILEGE OF WITNESSING YOUR SWORDPLAY? GOOD PEOPLE, DO YOU NOT WISH TO SEE THE GREATEST SWORDSWOMAN OF THE SIXTH GRADE?

HUZZAH!

LOOK, I THINK THEY'RE PUTTING ON A SHOW.

I DON'T HAVE MY SWORD.

HERE, TAKE MINE.

HEY! CAN I BORROW YOUR SWORD REAL QUICK? C'MON! I'LL GIVE IT BACK!

AND NOW, GOOD PEOPLE, PREPARE TO BE AMAZED! LADY ANITA, DOST THOU ACCEPT MY CHALLENGE?

IT'S REALLY HARD TO TURN DOWN A GOOD SWORD FIGHT WITH A FORMIDABLE OPPONENT.

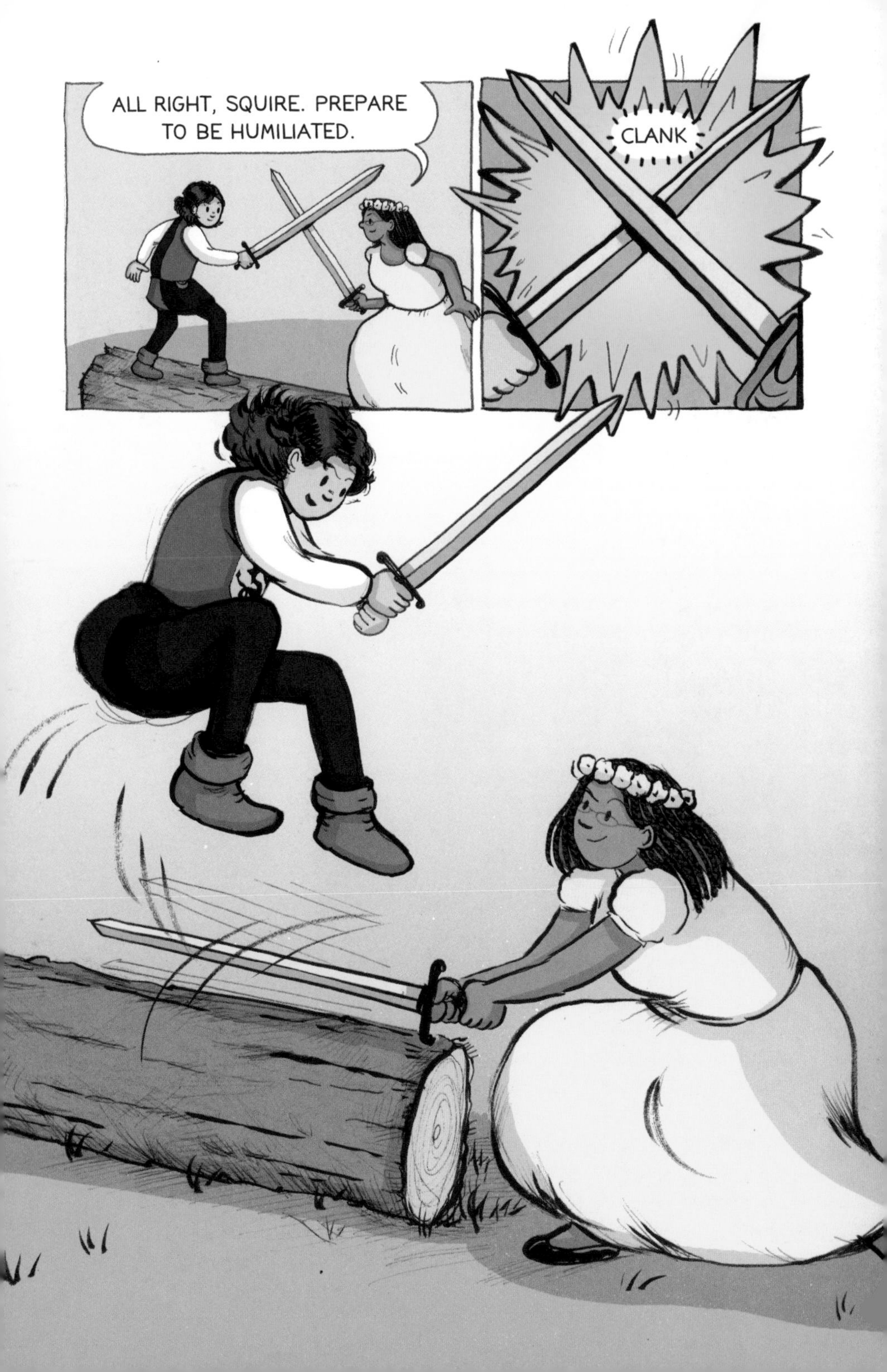
ALL RIGHT, SQUIRE. PREPARE TO BE HUMILIATED.
CLANK

AFTER WEEKS OF SPARRING WITH ANITA, I KNEW HER MOVES... AND HER WEAKNESSES.

WHEN SHE SWINGS TO HER LEFT, IT LEAVES HER RIGHT SIDE OPEN TO ATTACK.

ALL I HAD TO DO WAS THRUST...

STEP

AHA! LADY IMOGENE, I HAVE BESTED YOU. DO YOU CEDE THIS FIGHT?

I DO.

DO YOU CEDE THIS FIGHT?

PLEASE.

AYE. I DO CEDE THIS FIGHT, AND SHALL PUT OUR PAST DIFFERENCES BEHIND US.

NO HUGGING. YOU'RE ALL DIRTY.

HUZZAH!

HUZZAH!

THE CROWD SEEMED TO LIKE THE SHOW. SOME PEOPLE EVEN CAME UP FOR AUTOGRAPHS. NO TIPS, THOUGH.

THE KIDS FROM SCHOOL SEEMED TO LIKE IT.

WOW—THAT WAS AWESOME!

DO YOU TAKE LESSONS OR SOMETHING?

...EXCEPT FOR A CERTAIN SOMEONE.

I **KNEW** YOU WOULD FIND A WAY TO RUIN MY PARTY. YOU'RE **SUCH** A JERK.

C'MON, MIKA. I WASN'T TRYING TO RUIN YOUR PARTY. IT WAS A GOOD SHOW! MAYBE WE CAN START OVER. TRUCE?

YEAH, SURE.

TRUCE!

KICK

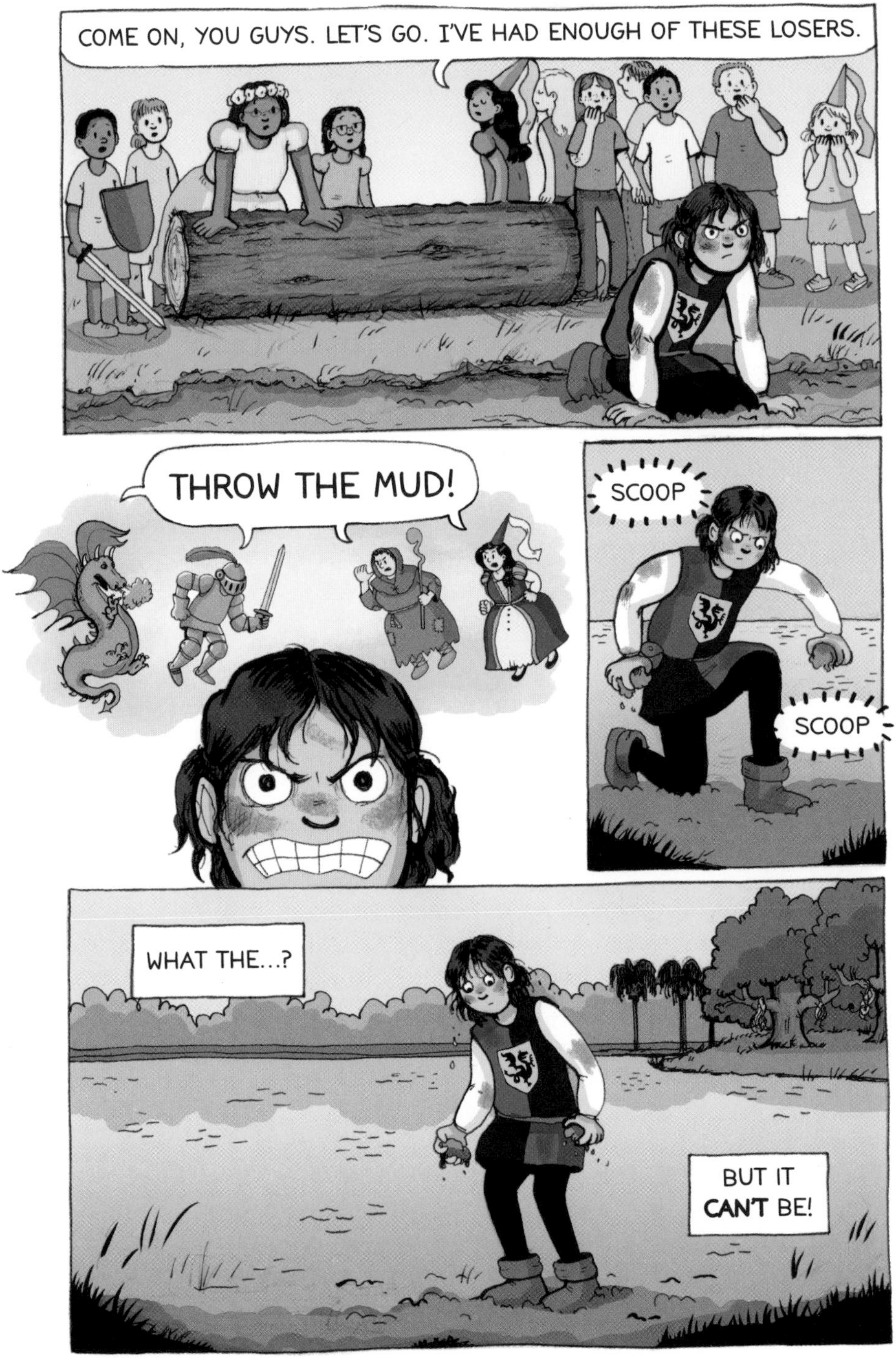
COME ON, YOU GUYS. LET'S GO. I'VE HAD ENOUGH OF THESE LOSERS.
THROW THE MUD!
SCOOP
SCOOP
WHAT THE...?
BUT IT **CAN'T** BE!

HARK! YOU CANNOT BEFOUL THIS WONDROUS DAY WITH YOUR CRUEL ACTIONS, YOU STALE OLD MOUSE-EATEN DRY CHEESE. FOR GOOD NEWS IS UPON US!

TIFFANY IS FOUND!

WHAT ARE YOU TALKING ABOUT?

I HAVE TO FIND FELIX! KNIGHTS-IN-TRAINING, COME ON!

FELIX!

FELIX!

FOR YEARS AFTERWARD, PEOPLE WOULD CALL ME THE SQUIRREL PIED PIPER, BECAUSE SOON IT SEEMED LIKE THE ENTIRE FAIRE WAS FOLLOWING ME.

WHAT'S GOING ON?

FELIX!

SHE FOUND THIS DIRTY SOCK IN THE MUD AND STARTED YELLING.

I THINK IT'S A SHOW.

THERE WAS ONLY ONE PLACE HE COULD BE.

GOOD SIR, I COMMITTED A GRAVE AND TERRIBLE MISTAKE WHEN I LOST YOUR FAITHFUL COMPANION, TIFFANY. THESE PAST FEW WEEKS HAVE BEEN LONG AND DIFFICULT, BUT AT LONG LAST, SHE IS FOUND AGAIN.

OK!

TIFFANY!

GOOD CITIZENS! THIS IS A WONDROUS DAY INDEED. OUR DEAR FRIEND TIFFANY HAS BEEN FOUND! I HEREBY DECLARE THAT TODAY SHALL BE KNOWN AS THE FEAST DAY OF ST. TIFFANY!

AND YOU, LADY IMOGENE, HAVE PROVEN THYSELF A SQUIRE WHO SERVES MY KINGDOM WELL WITH YOUR BRAVERY. SIR FELIX, LADY IMOGENE—I WOULD BE HONORED IF YOU JOINED ME IN LEADING THE ROYAL PROCESSION.

I DIDN'T BOTHER LOOKING FOR MIKA, OR SASHA, OR JASON—AND I DIDN'T CARE WHAT THEY THOUGHT. THEY WEREN'T IMPORTANT RIGHT NOW.

I WAS WITH MY FAIRE-MILY.

STILL, I COULDN'T HELP BUT NOTICE THE BLACK KNIGHT'S CHEERING SECTION AT THE JOUST...

AND EVEN THOUGH I JUST PICKED UP HORSE POOP AND DIDN'T GET TO BE IN THE BIG SWORD FIGHT, IT DIDN'T REALLY MATTER. THERE WAS ALWAYS NEXT YEAR.

HEY! THERE'S IMOGENE! LOOK, SHE'S IN THE SHOW! IMOGENE! HEY!

PLUS, THESE KIDS SEEMED LIKE THEY WERE EASILY IMPRESSED.

MIKA STAYED FAR AWAY...

YOU COULD HAVE BEEN, LIKE, TRAMPLED BY A HORSE!

YOU'RE LIKE A PROFESSIONAL ACTRESS!

BUT IT WAS LIKE VIOLET SAID. I GUESS NOT EVERYONE IN LIFE WAS GOING TO LIKE ME.

HERE COMES JASON! HE SAID HE HAD TO BUY SOMETHING...

MAYBE HE BOUGHT ME A **ROSE**! ...NO, THAT'S STUPID. I DON'T EVEN **WANT** HIM TO GET ME A ROSE....**DO I**?! WHAT'S THE MATTER WITH ME?!

AS OF TODAY I'VE SURVIVED TWO MONTHS OF MIDDLE SCHOOL, MIKA'S BIRTHDAY PARTY, AND ONE REAL SWORD-FIGHTING SHOW IN FRONT OF A CROWD. **AND** TIFFANY WAS BACK.

I'D CALL TODAY A SUCCESS.

THE LAST DAY OF FAIRE IS ALWAYS BITTERSWEET. BUT MOSTLY BITTER. IT WAS SO SAD TO THINK THIS WAS THE LAST PARADE...THE LAST CHESS MATCH...THE LAST NINE MEN'S MORRIS FOR A WHOLE YEAR.

BUT GUESS WHO SHOWED UP ON THE LAST DAY? SASHA!

I TOLD MY PARENTS HOW FUN IT WAS, AND THEY SAID WE COULD COME BACK TODAY!

I INTRODUCED HER TO EVERYBODY, AND TAUGHT HER HOW TO PLAY NINE MEN'S MORRIS.

MY PARENTS GAVE ME SOME MONEY...YOU WANT TO SHARE AN APPLE DUMPLING?

THOU ART SPEAKING MY LANGUAGE, SASHA!

ALL GOOD THINGS MUST COME TO AN END, THOUGH, AND BEFORE I KNEW IT THE GATES WERE CLOSING.

SEE YOU TOMORROW! I MEAN, ON THE MORROW!

THE CLOSING PARTY IS JUST FOR FAIRE-MILY...
WHICH SEEMS TO GROW BIGGER EACH YEAR.

AFTER THE GATES CLOSE, WE
ALL GO DOWN TO THE LAKE FOR
FAREWELL SONGS, DANCING,
EATING, AND DRINKING.

WHEN IT GETS DARK, WE DO MY VERY FAVORITE FAIRE TRADITION.
HISTORICALLY, IT WAS DONE DURING MIDSUMMER, NOT LATE OCTOBER,
BUT WE DON'T WORRY TOO MUCH ABOUT THE DETAILS.

FIRST, ALL THE LIGHTS ARE TURNED OFF.

THEN EVERYONE LIGHTS A CANDLE, MAKES A WISH, AND SETS IT ON THE LAKE. IT'S THE MOST BEAUTIFUL THING I'VE EVER SEEN.

I'VE HAD ENOUGH OF THIS LAKE FOR A WHILE, SO WHEN I LIGHT MY CANDLE I DON'T MAKE A WISH—I JUST WHISPER,

THANK YOU.

HEY FELIX. YOU WANT TO SIT UP HERE WITH ME?

SCOOCH

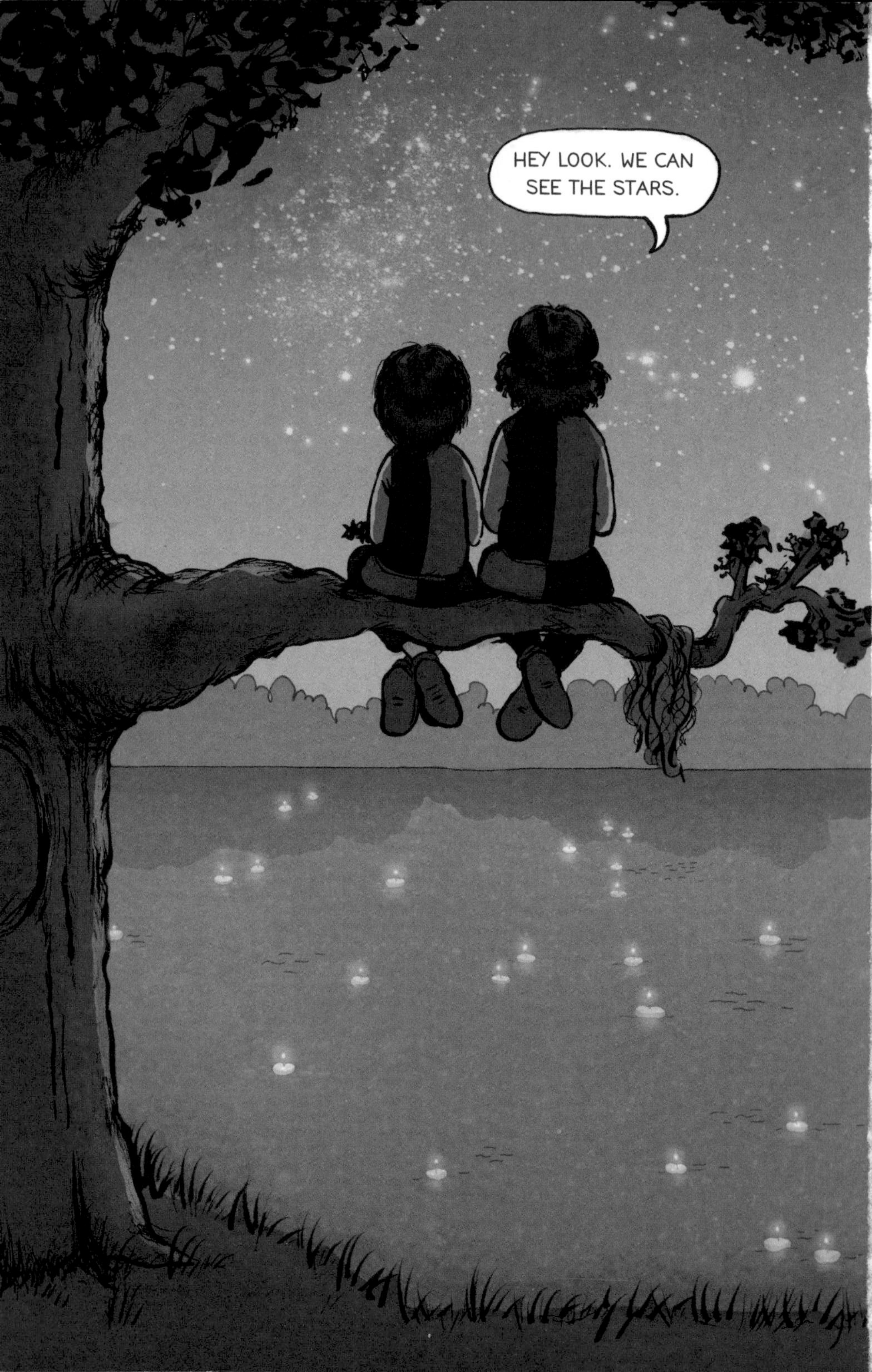
HEY LOOK. WE CAN SEE THE STARS.